AFTER JODIE

AFTER JODIE

Barbara Whitnell

This first world edition published in Great Britain 2005 by
SEVERN HOUSE PUBLISHERS LTD of
9–15 High Street, Sutton, Surrey SM1 1DF.
This first world edition published in the USA 2005 by
SEVERN HOUSE PUBLISHERS INC of
595 Madison Avenue, New York, N.Y. 10022.

British Library Cataloguing in Publication Data

Whitnell, Barbara
  After Jodie
  1.   Single mothers - England - Cornwall - Fiction
  2.   Cornwall (England) - Fiction
  3.   Suspense fiction
  I.   Title
  823.9'14 [F]

  ISBN-10 : 0-7278-6266-9

Typeset by Palimpsest Book Production Ltd.,
Polmont, Stirlingshire, Scotland.
Printed and bound in Great Britain by
MPG Books Ltd., Bodmin, Cornwall.

One

I must have been the last one in the village to hear about Jodie.

It was a glorious day – early March and the first intimation of spring we'd had for ages. It was also the first time for longer than I could remember that I'd felt that lift of the spirits which only comes after a long and dismal winter, during which it seems that sunshine and blue sky and skipping lambs are no more than figments of the imagination, never to be seen again.

I felt, that day, almost euphoric. The sea was sparkling so brightly that it almost hurt the eyes to look at it, and there were early primroses and violets in the hedgerows.

Jamie, from the fastness of his buggy, reached out to try to grab them as I pushed him down the hill towards the cluster of roofs and the crouching church tower that was the tiny fishing village of Trenellack. He'd slept during the morning and had woken up full of energy and demanding entertainment, so I'd zipped him into his little red windcheater, passed on to me by my friend and landlady Mary Trembath, and set out.

On that wonderful day I'd been less daunted by the thought of the hill that lay before me than was sometimes the case – a hill that was long enough on the way down and seemed twice as long on the way back. Normally I found it easier to catch the bus at the end of the lane and go to the supermarket in St Venn. This had the advantage

1

of being cheaper than Mrs Jago's shop, too, though I suffered pangs of guilt; I was fully aware that, when it comes to village shops, we use them or lose them. I was, however, in no state to be altruistic about such things. Counting pennies was an essential part of my day-to-day life, the finding of buy-one-get-one-free deals small but distinct triumphs.

But today I exulted in the walk. It was the sort of day that encouraged hope and made me certain that things would get better; that Jamie would grow up healthy and happy and that my finances would improve in some miraculous way, and that I would shed the lingering misery of past failures. I felt, that day, lucky to live in such a beautiful place, lucky to have good friends and good health, a roof over my head and a bright little boy.

I picked a primrose and put it in Jamie's chubby fist.

'Primrose,' I said.

'F'ower,' he corrected me. He sniffed at it and grinned up at me. 'Nice.'

'Very nice,' I agreed. 'It's a flower called a primrose.'

He considered the word and appeared to be trying it for size. Then he grinned again.

'I say "f'ower",' he said firmly; then, his attention caught by the sheep with their lambs in the field we were passing, he forgot about such botanical niceties and began singing 'Baa Baa Black Sheep', accompanied by a vigorous bouncing action which made me fear for the future of the buggy, already long past its first youth – having, yet again, been passed on from Mary. Like everything else, it had been gratefully accepted.

Having achieved the village, accompanied all the way by Jamie's rendition of 'The Grand Old Duke of York' and 'Hickory Dickory Dock' among other snatches of song, I unbuckled him and held his hand as he climbed laboriously up the steps to the shop where Mrs Jago had ruled the roost for as long as I could remember. My mother had taken me there, just as I was taking Jamie, and later Jodie and I had spent our Saturday pocket money on sherbet dips and acid drops, gobstoppers and liquorish whirls.

Mrs Jago was a short, fat, good-natured lady who had always seemed middle-aged to me, though of course she must have been quite a young woman in those far-off days. She was always cheerfully garrulous and I felt sure of a welcome from her, as was her custom. Her smile was strained, however, her demeanour somehow suggesting that on this occasion cheerfulness was out of the question, and at the sight of me her mouth trembled as if she was about to be overcome with emotion.

'Oh, Prue, my dear, you poor little maid,' she said compassionately. 'You must be that upset. Well, aren't we all? 'Tis awful, that's what 'tis.'

'What's happened?' I asked her, totally lost.

'You haven't heard about Jodie? Surely, you must have!'

My best friend. My oldest friend. We'd been inseparable throughout our childhood at the village school and had moved up to St Venn Grammar School together. We hadn't seen quite so much of each other since her marriage to Tom, but she sometimes dropped by the cottage on her way home from work, and over tea we'd exchange confidences or laugh hysterically at very little, just as we always had. Life had always been a joke to Jodie and she never failed to cheer and divert me. At school, I was always in trouble for it, being often reduced to helpless giggles whilst she had this uncanny knack of being able to keep a perfectly straight face. I cannot describe what a support she had been to me all the previous year.

'What about Jodie?' It couldn't be anything really bad, I thought. Not *really* bad. Not Jodie.

'She's dead, my handsome. Killed herself.'

I stared at her, not able to take it in.

'*Killed herself?* What on earth do you mean? She'd never do that!'

'No, no – not killed herself. I didn't mean that.' Distractedly she flapped a hand in front of her face. ''Twas an accident, like. Up there on the path when she was coming back from work.' She gave a jerk of her head, indicating the direction of the sea and the cliffs and the path that Jodie took when she walked to and from Boscothey Manor, the hotel where she worked. 'There was that cliff fall the other week, see, and 'twasn't safe. The council had fenced it off and she should never have come that way. She should have known better. Oh, the silly girl,' she added, in a tone full of regretful affection.

'She did know,' I said. I knew that for a certainty. The last time I'd seen her had been about ten days before, and she'd mentioned the cliff fall then. It was a nuisance, she said, because she walked home that way whenever Tom needed the car, unless she intended dropping in to see me, when she would take the path through the fields. That was a much longer way home, however, and so was the road, which wound this way and that. Now, until it was made safe, it was out of the question to go via the cliffs. She had to take the long way home, with or without the car.

'She decided to risk it, I s'pose. 'Twas late last evening they found her. Tom got anxious when she didn't come back at the usual time. He phoned Boscothey and they said she'd left long before, so he went looking for her.'

'Poor Tom. Oh, poor Tom!' My heart had been so full of my own shock that for a moment I'd lost sight of how much greater Tom's must have been. They'd been married only a couple of years and were devoted to each other. Hoping to start a family, Jodie had confided to me.

'Mummy, Mummy, Mummy. Sweeties, Mummy.'

Jamie was tugging my hand, pulling me over to the sweet counter. Abstractedly I took a small fruit lolly from a jar, unwrapped it and handed it to him. The usual considerations regarding sticky windcheaters and tooth decay never entered my mind.

'She usually took the car,' I said.

Mrs Jago took on an air of self-importance as she leaned a little further over the counter towards me. She was the one who had all the insider knowledge and despite her grief, which I felt sure was very real, part of her, I could see, was relishing the moment.

'Tom feels that bad about it,' she said. 'He needed the car yesterday for his work, see. He dropped her off at Boscothey in the morning but she said she'd find her own way home. He never thought she'd go by the cliff. Well, you wouldn't, would you? 'Tisn't all that far by the road, after all. Devastated, he is, the poor young man. Devastated.'

All my joy in the day had evaporated. I felt winded, hollow with grief and anger that such a vibrant, beautiful, funny person as Jodie had been snuffed out by what, probably, had been just a momentary, impulsive decision to save a few minutes by taking the short-cut home no matter what the dangers. I couldn't blame her. We both knew those cliffs like the backs of our hands and had climbed over most of them when we were young. And she'd always been a daredevil, I remembered, accomplishing feats that I'd been too fearful to attempt.

'They say there's to be an inquest,' Mrs Jago went on.

'Well, there's bound to be, I s'pose, though everyone can see with half an eye 'twas nothing but an accident. "Death by misadventure",' she added, a touch portentously.

I nodded in agreement. Of course it was an accident. What else could it have been? The alternatives were limited, after all.

'I suppose formalities have to be gone through,' I said, 'even if the verdict is cut and dried. It's hard on Tom, though.'

I could hardly remember what I'd come to the shop for in the first place, but in the end collected my wits sufficiently to buy a few things, though I only remembered chilli powder when I was halfway up the hill. But what did chilli powder matter in the face of a tragedy like this? Nothing much seemed to matter when the picture of Jodie, smashed on the granite rocks under the cliff, was before me and could not be dismissed.

Jodie's mother, who had moved to Truro to be near her sister after the death of her husband, had come back to Trenellack to look after Tom, Mrs Jago had told me. I was glad of that. Mrs Bailey had always been fond of Tom and the feeling was reciprocated, so perhaps they were able to comfort each other. Perhaps. Somehow I felt it would be a long, long time before Tom was comforted by anything.

He and Jodie had known each other from childhood and though there were four years between them they'd always been mates, always been aware of each other. I hadn't been at all surprised when this feeling had ripened into something stronger, though it had taken its time. After university, Jodie had moved to London and worked for a while as a researcher for an MP, during which time she had sown a few wild oats in and around Westminster.

Tom, meanwhile, had become a surveyor, had married

– disastrously – and had returned to Cornwall after the divorce to make a new life for himself. He joined a firm of surveyors in St Venn, bought an old fisherman's cottage down by the quay in Trenellack and renovated it, bought a boat, became part of the scene. Jodie, returning from time to time to see her mother and breathe some country air, was soon perceived to be heading west more frequently, while Tom, hitherto apparently quite satisfied with the entertainment Cornwall had to offer, now sometimes went to London for the weekend.

Almost the whole of the village came to the wedding. Kit and I were still together in those days and Jamie was just a tiny newborn baby. Even then I suppose I knew that my own marriage was in trouble, but I hadn't given it up for lost. Our chosen way of life meant a lot of stress and hard work, which in itself created problems, but I was still determined to make a success of the marriage and I thought Kit was too.

So there was a poignant kind of sweetness in hearing Tom and Jodie make their vows. I looked up at Kit, catching his eye and smiling as they repeated the ancient words, hoping that he'd remember that we had made the same kind of promises. He was smiling too, but bitterly, cynically.

'Poor sod,' he whispered, and for a moment it seemed as if the light streaming in through the stained-glass windows had dimmed; I turned away from him, suddenly more fearful for our future.

I'd met Kit Ryder in Exeter, where I was working for a firm of estate agents, having discovered the hard way that an English degree doesn't necessarily prepare a girl for becoming one of life's movers and shakers. I learned to type and use a computer, which at least made me employable, but I had the distinct feeling that I was marking time, waiting for something to happen that would show me just what I ought to do with my life. One thing I was certain of: working for an estate agent wasn't it.

I still had friends in Exeter from my time at the university, and it was through them that I met Kit. He was tall, dark and, though not conventionally handsome, had the kind of magnetism that I, for one, found irresistible. He was also an artist who seldom sold any paintings and was perpetually broke. But what, I asked myself, did money matter? He had great talent, bucketloads of charm, and the kind of self-belief that made me certain he would make it to the top one day.

No one could be more charming, more quirkily endearing, than Kit. Other men might text or phone the object of their affections. He posted little love notes and invitations through my door, copiously illustrated with swiftly drawn sketches – things such as a knight saving a maiden from a dragon, or fighting a duel for a lady's honour, or swooning at the sight of her beauty.

Friends told me he was self-absorbed and unreliable – the sort of man who would shy away from any form of commitment – but I didn't believe them. They didn't understand him, I thought to myself. Not like me.

We all had pasts, I said lightly, when I learned of the girls he had loved and left. This thing between Kit and me was different. I adored him from the moment of our meeting and felt sure – well, almost sure – that he loved me too.

It was a bad time for me in other ways. My father had died at sea in the Falklands when I was five and my mother brought me up alone. It wasn't too hard a life – modest but reasonably comfortable. There weren't many luxuries, but we got by well enough. She had a navy pension and we lived in a substantial Victorian house on one of the hills leading out of Trenellack. Apart from the lack of a father, it was a blissfully happy childhood, with the Cornish cliffs and beaches as my playground and a mother who was a positive, unjudgemental kind of influence. She saw the best in everyone – especially, it has to be said, her only daughter. And eventually, disastrously, in Kit.

She was terminally ill at the time I met Kit, and I was going down to Cornwall almost every weekend until I realised the utter impossibility of keeping it up. Because of Kit, I probably delayed leaving Exeter longer than I should have done, but at last I saw there was no alternative but to hand in my notice and move back to Trenellack to look after my mother properly for her last weeks or months, however long it proved to be. Most likely weeks, the doctor said.

It was then, soon after I arrived home, that I began feeling very sick in the mornings, took a test and found I was pregnant. My first instinct was to keep it quiet, not to worry my mother about it, but late one night when she couldn't rest and we had been sitting and talking about our lives, I found I couldn't hold out any longer.

She told me she'd suspected as much for some time.

'What on earth made you do that?' I asked.

'Well, you do look a bit peaky, darling, and I'm pretty sure that you've been sick several times the last few mornings. Don't forget I'm next to the bathroom. And the way you talk about Kit makes me sure that you're sleeping with him. I'm not too ill or too daft to put two and two together.'

I sighed. 'Yes, of course I'm sleeping with him, but I don't know why I'm pregnant. I always took precautions.'

'You never relied on him?'

'No – oh, yes! Just one weekend when we got caught

away from home and stayed in Bath with a friend of his. Are you shocked?'

She considered the matter.

'No, not shocked. I don't think in my present circumstances there's much could shock me. Anyway, you clearly love him.' She gave a brief laugh, for in spite of everything she still found things to laugh at. 'Mind you, I don't know what your grandmother would have said.'

My grandmother had been called Prudence and had been the archetypical virtuous Methodist, a pillar of the local chapel and an example to all. I'm not sure if I was named after her because my parents liked the name or because they hoped that I would inherit her unimpeachable nature. I hardly needed a diagram to see that, if the latter, then I had fallen short. I sighed.

'I regret that prudence has nothing to do with it,' I said.

My mother laughed again.

'No,' she said. 'I agree with you there. Have you told Kit yet?'

'Not yet. I don't know how he'll take it.'

'He must be told. It's only fair, Prue, both to you and to him. You say he loves you—'

'Well, I think he does, but a baby . . .! I can't see him welcoming the idea.'

'He must be given a chance. He must know.'

'I don't want to pressurise him.'

'Well, think about it. I'm sure you'll decide I'm right.'

Kit came down the next weekend and I told him then. As I had feared, he wasn't at all pleased, but the next day he appeared to have thought it over and changed his position. Easy now to think, cynically, that he'd taken a look at the house, and my mother's closeness to death, and had decided that matters could be worse. At least the mother of his child would own what was now quite a valuable piece of real estate. Whatever his reasons, he proposed marriage and I gladly accepted.

My mother was totally charmed by him, as I knew she would be, and was quite sure we were doing the right thing, no matter that he didn't have a penny to bless himself with.

'He has a way with him,' she said. 'And he makes you laugh, darling, which is something that can't be under-estimated. He's talented, too, and full of ambition – and you know, darling, he does love you so. He told me so this morning when we had our little chat. I shall go much happier knowing that you've got him to support you, mentally and physically if not financially. It's no fun bringing up a child on your own, and success will come, I'm sure.'

I did say that she saw the best in everyone; which isn't the same as saying she was a good judge of char-acter. However, with her approval we married, just a week before she died, and indeed it did make her very happy. And I was happy – and Kit appeared to be so too.

The house, of course, was left to me. It had four good bedrooms and a huge attic and Kit came up with the idea of converting it into a guest-house.

'It would cost a fortune,' I said, though I was never-theless intrigued by the idea. I liked cooking, liked look-ing after people. And I'd loved being back in Trenellack.

Kit was enthusiastic.

'We could borrow against the house, run the business as a team. Off season, I could paint. There are plenty of galleries in St Venn and Truro where I could sell my stuff.'

It seemed, suddenly, the best of ideas. Tom came round, surveyed the place and told us what needed doing. All the bedrooms were big enough to have a small slice cut off for an en suite shower room, and the huge attic could be converted to a small flat for the two of us – or, in a mere six months' time, the three of us.

A wonderful theory, which all got under way quite quickly, the council granting us planning permission in what everyone said was record time.

I will gloss over the disruption and the noise and mess and the making of endless cups of tea for the builders, and the way everything seemed to cost more than we had expected, and the fact that we had to camp in one room while everything was being done. This was just par for the course and it was nothing we weren't able to take in our stride. I found it exciting, stimulating, and I never stopped making plans for our forthcoming guest-house. It was going to be the last word in comfort and good taste.

What I did not expect was the rapidity with which any form of support from Kit was withdrawn. He soon made it clear that he found me a turn-off as my pregnancy burgeoned. He began to drink too much, which worried me, not only because it made him difficult to live with but also because, although the building society loan had come through, the cost of the construction work seemed to escalate by the minute and it was essential that we kept our living costs as low as possible.

Every night he wanted to go to the Ship Inn and stay till closing time, but although I went with him at first, the smoky atmosphere and the smell of beer made me feel nauseous and I stopped going. I couldn't stand the late nights, either. In fact, according to Kit, this baby was the worst thing that had ever happened to either of us and I must have been damned careless to let it happen. Prudence! What a joke!

I reflected, from time to time, on the fact that my mother thought he made me laugh. Well, he had done in the beginning, but now there was no more charm on his part, no more love notes or cartoons. Just coldness and boredom and surliness, and total lack of interest in the coming baby. He said, many times, that I should have had an abortion while there was time.

'But this is your son,' I said, for by then we knew the baby's sex. 'And he's alive and moving and our responsibility. How can you say something like that?'

'Because it's a responsibility I don't need and never asked for,' was his reply.

It was stress that was making him like this, I told myself, and I went on letting him manage the money and take care of the bills, which later proved to be one of my more foolish acts, and yet one more way in which I belied my name; however, I believed his assurances that all was going to plan and we had enough in hand. It never occurred to me to doubt him because the whole venture had been his idea from the beginning and I thought he was as much behind it as I was.

One lives and learns. When the time came for Jamie to be born, I went in the ambulance to St Venn on my own, for Kit was too drunk to care. And all the time I had the vague idea that it was my fault; that I wasn't making enough effort to keep myself attractive, or involve him enough in making decisions about the fixtures and fittings. When the baby came, I kept telling myself, it would all be different. I'd be slim again, more active, we'd be a family, and Kit's attitude towards him would change. Maybe he would prove to look like his dad and Kit wouldn't be able to help loving him.

But it wasn't like that. Kit could hardly bear to look at our son, let alone hold him or do anything for him. He hated the inevitable disruption to our lives, though heaven knows Jamie cried very little compared to some babies I had known. And it was quite impossible to tell whom he resembled. Some said he was like Kit, others that he was just like my mother. He was a bit scrawny, I had to admit. I couldn't see any likeness to anyone.

Kit stayed out more, his temper more uncertain by the day. Gone completely was the charming young man who had bedazzled both me and my mother. And it was then I discovered that the mortgage hadn't been paid for three months and that the builders were still owed thousands of pounds that Kit had squandered or salted away somewhere. I'd been a fool to trust him, that much was clear. Why hadn't I recognised the full extent of his betrayal? I'd been too busy, I suppose, or too lazy, or too full of dreams.

Inevitably there was a showdown and he slammed out of the house, leaving me and Trenellack behind, as well as his collection of canvases and brushes gathering dust in the garden shed. And the bills rolled in: for water and electricity and Council Tax, never mind the builders and the painter and the plumber and the credit cards. And the Ship Inn. They'd been putting his drinks on the slate for weeks. He had robbed us all blind and I had no idea where he had gone or what had happened to the money he should have paid out.

In the end there was no alternative but to sell, and this I had done, though I could hardly believe the small amount of capital that was left once I had paid all the outstanding accounts. The Trembaths came to my rescue. Mary and Roger were old friends who farmed just outside Trenellack. There was a tiny, unoccupied cottage on their land, once used by one of the farm workers but now lying empty. They were thinking of renovating it to make guest accommodation, since farmers had to diversify to survive these days, but they weren't in a hurry and were happy to let me have it for next to no rent while they considered their options and sought the required planning permission.

'It's no great shakes but it'll give you breathing space,' Mary said. And it had done. There was a kitchen and living room on the ground floor with a steep staircase going up to two small bedrooms and a bathroom. I'd spent the winter there and had grown quite attached to the place. It was basically sound, despite the antiquity of the kitchen, and once its draughts were dealt with and the whole place was cleaned up and repainted it had a certain charm. It had a little garden, fore and aft, and although otherwise isolated was only a couple of hundred yards from the Trembaths' farmhouse. The views across the valley to the sea were something that people paid thousands for, and it was no small consolation that I had it almost for free.

The day I heard about Jodie, I certainly needed consolation. As I pushed the buggy back up the hill, not singing this time and finding it hard to respond to Jamie's conversational overtures, I thought about Jodie and I thought about me, and I remembered those two happy, heedless girls who had shopped for sweeties together and explored the cliffs and picnicked on the beach and swum in the sea and gone on the school bus to St Venn. Later we'd swapped boyfriends and clothes and confidences and danced to the record player in Jodie's front room, copying the latest stars on *Top of the Pops*. There had been times, of course, when we'd fallen out. Everyone has faults, and I'm in no way absolving myself, but Jodie had a hot temper that occasionally got out of hand. We were both pretty headstrong, both liked our own way, but no rows lasted long. Jodie could keep up a quarrel longer than I could; I missed her company too much not to give in, but she'd make up for it by the generosity of her capitulation.

'Baa baa, black sheep,' sang Jamie. '*Sing*, Mummy.'

We'd reached the field with the sheep again. I forced a smile, but couldn't quite bring myself to start singing.

'Soon be home,' I said. It was the only consolation I could think of.

Two

It was a pity about the chilli powder, because Ian Channing was coming to supper and he was very partial to chilli. Well, it couldn't be helped, and what did it matter anyway, in the light of the news about Jodie? Shepherd's pie would do equally well.

Ian, in any case, wasn't coming primarily to eat. He had offered to put up some badly needed shelves in the kitchen and I had thankfully accepted. There was nothing more to it than that – not on my part, anyway. He was a good friend and very handy with the Black & Decker. I wasn't in the market for anything else, even though I was sometimes aware of that certain glint in his eye when he looked at me. I pretended to ignore it, though in a way I was grateful for it. It made me feel as if I wasn't altogether undesirable, even if, paradoxically, I didn't want anyone to desire me.

As eyes go, Ian's were rather good, I had to admit: an attractive dark grey, set in a squarish, blunt-featured face. He wasn't handsome in the least, but he was intelligent and made me laugh, which was something that I was very grateful for. There hadn't been a lot to laugh at in the previous year.

He was also utterly reliable. Maybe that was his trouble, I sometimes thought. Maybe there was something in me that was attracted to the unconventional rotter. Ian, with his promising career and his *bijou* town house in Truro and his sleek and spotless BMW, was far from that; yet I knew it was wrong to dismiss him as a yuppy, not interested in anything but the material. Sometimes I would have a thought, hear an argument, and would think: I wonder what Ian would say about that? We could talk endlessly – about books, politics, ideas generally – yet I knew I put up barriers all the time. I'd lost all confidence when it came to men and the last thing I wanted was to get too close to anyone. I didn't want to be that vulnerable; couldn't, in fact, entertain the thought of sharing my life, my bed, my all with any man.

He was Mary Trembath's brother, six years older than me, and a partner in a firm of solicitors in Truro. I suppose that makes his DIY tendencies seem a little unexpected, but according to Mary he had always been that way inclined and though he liked his new town house and found it very convenient, he was also frustrated because there was simply nothing he could do to it. He seemed only too pleased to take out this frustration on my cottage, and I was equally pleased to accept his help. Since we'd become reacquainted at Mary's birthday party the previous year, he had hung a new front door for me, plumbed in a washing machine, helped me scrape off the truly revolting wallpaper in the sitting room and paint it white, and replaced a rotten floorboard in my bedroom. He'd also given me some free legal advice regarding a possible divorce. It couldn't happen yet because nobody had the slightest idea where Kit was to be found, but there were only three or so years to go before I could divorce him anyway. Ian said he would keep the matter under review, and I had every faith in him.

Mary, who tended to take the mickey out of Ian's conventionality and predictability as only a sister can, rather hoped, I think, that we would get it together. She and I were good friends despite the difference in our circumstances, as were Jamie and her little boy, William. She'd had a baby girl, Jess, four months ago and had confided to me that she had every intention of having at least two more before she would consider her family complete. But don't tell Roger, she'd said to me.

Roger complained constantly that times were hard, farming in the doldrums, etc. etc., but compared to mine the lifestyle at Hollybush Farm was positively lavish. The farmhouse was old but had been beautifully modernised in those days when farmers were enjoying a bonanza. The kitchen was a dream, with an Aga and a big farmhouse table just made for a family, and in the sitting room there was a big stone inglenook and deep, comfortable chairs. There were always plenty of books about too, and flowers, and bottles in the drinks cabinet. Mary had her own little car, a Metro, and a constant supply of cute and colourful garments arrived from her mother for young William, now aged three. I didn't begrudge them any of it. They worked hard and had been good to me.

But how different, I mused sometimes, from the home life of Prudence Ryder. I had come to the sad realisation that I was in what is generally known as the poverty trap and seemed incapable of clambering out of it. The difficulty of finding a suitable job was matched only by the difficulty of finding anyone to look after Jamie; anyone I could afford, anyway. I had no car to ferry him to a nursery and because this was some way out of the village, public transport wasn't an option either.

But at least I was alive, I reminded myself. Not like dear Jodie. Thoughts about the tragedy kept sweeping over me and each time I felt sadder and sicker than before. How could it possibly have happened? She knew of the dangers of cliff falls and crumbling paths; we'd seen them often enough in the past and despite her daring nature we always treated them with respect, ever since, at the age of ten or so, I had nearly come to grief when we were scrambling on the cliffs above Boscothey beach. Not far, now I came to think about it, from the place where Jodie must have fallen so recently.

Ian arrived on the dot of seven, which was exactly when he said he would come, and as usual he was bearing a bottle of my favourite Australian wine. I told him about Jodie, but not until we were at the table eating our shepherd's pie. I waited until then because I'd wanted to get Jamie in bed and out of the way before discussing it, and in addition had no wish to compete with the noise of the drill which Ian had been employing non-stop from the moment of his arrival.

Ian stared at me in horror at the news, fork halfway to his mouth.

'*Jodie?* My God, how dreadful! Why didn't you say? You must be devastated.'

'You could say so.'

'She was a lovely girl.'

'I know.'

'Her poor husband – Tom, isn't it? Remember, they both came up and pitched in when we were scraping off the wallpaper? They seemed so happy.'

'They were.'

'And you – she was your best friend. Prue, I'm so sorry.'

Suddenly I wanted, very much, to lay my head down on the table or on his shoulder, or practically anywhere, and weep. Until this moment, while I had Jamie to think of, I had suppressed the worst of my grief, but now Ian's words of sympathy seemed to unlock the floodgates.

I put down my knife and fork and stared down at my plate, desperately trying to stop the tears welling over. The next thing I knew, Ian was out of his chair and pressing my face into his warm woolly sweater while I sobbed helplessly.

It didn't last long. Soon I disentangled myself and reached for a tissue from a box on the dresser.

'Eat your supper,' I sniffed. 'It'll go cold.'

'Well, you drink your wine.'

I did so, gratefully, but only picked at the food on my plate. Ian's appetite, I noticed, seemed unimpaired – but then why should it not be? He'd only met Jodie on that one occasion. He had obviously taken to her, but could hardly be expected to feel as deeply as I did.

'You know what?' he said, when we had finished and I'd risen from the table to make coffee. 'You ought to get yourself over to Boscothey Manor and apply for Jodie's job. It would suit you down to the ground.'

The sheer heartlessness of it took my breath away.

'*What?*' I thumped the coffee pot down on the table. 'How can you be so . . .' I fumbled for the word, 'so—'

'"Insensitive" is the description you're looking for,' he said helpfully. 'Though I deny it absolutely. They'll take on someone to fill the gap Jodie's left, won't they? Why not you? She would hardly grudge you the chance, would she?'

I sat down heavily in my chair and looked at him across the table.

'Honestly, Ian, I hardly know what to say. You are so – so *practical*!'

It was, now I came to think about it, just the sort of reasonable, unemotional suggestion I would expect him to make under the circumstances; just the sort of matter-of-fact attitude that made him a successful, highly paid solicitor.

'And that's wrong in your book?'

'Well, in this case I can't think it's right. Not now. Not yet.'

'OK.' He shrugged. 'Forget I spoke. It's just that with Boscothey just five minutes' walk down the valley—'

'More than five minutes.'

He laughed at that. 'Seven, then. Well, ten. Whatever. You've got to admit it's handy. And you could do the job just as well as Jodie.'

'How do you know? She was a much better secretary than I ever was. And I'm not that well up in computer skills. I've used one, of course, but not for ages. I bet they've got all the latest technology down there. And anyway, what would Tom think?'

'I hardly imagine,' Ian said drily, 'that the extent of his grief is going to be affected by whatever you do. He'll have a little more on his mind than that. As for the technology – you'd pick it up in no time. You're rusty, that's all.'

'You're not kidding,' I agreed gloomily. But after all, I couldn't help toying with the idea. Was he right? Should I go for it? I did need the money, there were no two ways about that. But there was still the problem of Jamie. 'Of course,' I added with a touch of sarcasm, 'I'm sure they'd be delighted to welcome me, coming as I do with a twenty-two-month-old little boy as an attachment.'

'Have you spoken to Mary lately?'

'What's that got to do with it?'

'She's been asked to go back to her job at the hospital. They're desperately short of physios and say she can do any hours she wants.'

'So?'

'She'd love to do it, really, but of course there's William and Jess to consider. William could go to the nursery, but

Jess is too young so the only option is a nanny of some kind.'

'Good ones are hard to come by. And expensive.'

'Grace Polmear is looking for a job.'

'Grace? Oh, wow – you couldn't get anyone better.'

Everyone knew Grace. She was, I guess, in her fifties and had been part of the village scene for as long as I could remember. She had never married, but had stayed at home to look after her disabled father and provide a home, whenever called upon, for several nephews and nieces whose parents were abroad and who were at boarding school in Truro. Her father had died fairly recently and the nephews and nieces were growing up and now, I assumed, well able to fend for themselves.

'I told Mary she'd be mad not to grab her,' Ian said, and I nodded.

'Couldn't agree more.'

'If Mary takes her on, it strikes me that you could share her. Wouldn't that be a good idea? Split the cost?'

'Trust you to have it all worked out in a nanosecond!'

'It just seems such a practical arrangement. You'll never find a job nearer at hand.'

'I still think it's too soon.'

'Well, think some more.'

And I did. Almost all night. And of course, Ian was right. As always. Boscothey Manor stood in a kind of fold in the valley between Hollybush Farm and the sea, and as he'd said, it wasn't more than a ten-minute walk away. I could, in fact, see the top of one of the manor's turrets from my bedroom window.

I'd been down that path so many times in the past. The manor had been empty for a long time, a source of great interest to me in my romantic teenage years. I'd prowled around its deserted garden, peered in through the windows, mourned at its deterioration and woven many a fanciful story about it. Sometimes, when the mist drifted in from the sea, it seemed to float a little above the ground like some mythical fairy castle. I used to fantasise that I'd marry a millionaire and restore it to its former glory. And we'd live happily ever after, naturally.

Standing on what had been its front lawn, you could see a path leading straight ahead to Boscothey Cove. This was the only point of access to the beach, for both to the left and to the right the cliffs rose quite steeply. It was along the path to the west of the cove, halfway to Trenellack, that Jodie had fallen to her death.

In the eighteenth century, it was said, its hard-drinking owner, Sir Joseph Boscothey, was hanged at Bodmin Jail for the murder of a revenue man who had come to investigate reports of smuggling. It was easy to imagine even now the line of horses, plodding up the path from the beach, wreathed in mist, laden with brandy and silks, the clinking of their harnesses muffled with rags.

More recently, I remembered seeing Agnes Boscothey in the village when I was a child. She was the last of her line, an odd-looking woman, tall and thin, an anxious bespectacled spinster with a long red nose, much given to good works which went largely unappreciated by the village. She lived alone with her housekeeper and was considered something of a joke, poor woman, because of her abrupt, hectoring manner. Looking back, I feel sure she was merely lonely and rather shy, but nevertheless determined to do her duty towards the poorer members of society.

Inevitably she died, and thereafter the house stayed empty. For a while it was occupied by some kind of commune and it deteriorated rapidly; it was said they used the banisters and floorboards for firewood and kept hens in the kitchen, as well as indulging in strange practices that grew more frightening with every telling. True or not, everyone in the area was glad when they moved on and it was bought by an exclusive hotel chain which, after much repair and refurbishment, transformed it into a luxurious hideaway for the seriously rich.

'It'll bring trade to the village,' Mrs Jago had said to me with great satisfaction when it first opened. 'We're only a mile or so away, after all. It's got to make a difference, mark my words.'

It didn't, though, or not very much. A few villagers were employed to clean there and an elderly, slow-witted chap called Benny Bean was taken on as a handyman-cum-porter, and of course Jodie became a PA. Apart from that, the gardeners and the two receptionists were transferred from other hotels belonging to the chain and lived on site. The hotel bought its provisions elsewhere, apart from fish, which the chef bought direct from the fish market on the quay at St Venn. Few guests ever bothered to come to Trenellack. It was only a small hamlet with a shingly beach. Hotel guests had a swimming pool in the grounds, Boscothey beach on the doorstep, and if they wanted more, they were already halfway to St Venn in the opposite direction, which was a far more interesting place with its photogenic harbour and picturesque little streets as well as shops and restaurants of all kinds. The hotel motor boat, *Firefly*, was moored there too, and they had a special arrangement for the hiring of sailing boats from old Captain Toms.

Jodie had worked as secretary and PA for Paul and Delia Ransleigh, the joint managers, and though she complained to me a bit about Delia, who apparently could be demanding and irrational, she seemed to get on well

enough with Paul. He was, she said, a bit wet but otherwise OK. The job had suited her, I knew. Would it suit
me too?

Probably there was already a queue of women apply-
ing for it from St Venn and all points west, which would
make this heart-searching a complete waste of effort.
However, by the time dawn broke I'd decided that it
wouldn't hurt to have a word with Mary about childcare.
If it all worked out, at least I would be free to look for
a job elsewhere, even if I decided not to throw my hat in
the ring at Boscothey Manor.

It was Jodie's mother who persuaded me in the end. I
went to the village to drop a note of condolence into the
house which had seemed so filled with happiness such a
short time ago. I hadn't intended to intrude by knocking
at the door, but Mrs Bailey happened to meet me at the
front gate on her return from shopping and insisted on
my going in for a cup of coffee.

She seemed very calm and controlled. I think I was
more tearful than she was – but she was worried about
Tom, she said. He had said very little but was clearly
distraught, and seemed unable to grieve openly. He spent
most of the time isolated in the bedroom he used as a
study, was hardly eating at all but was drinking far too
much. He had insisted on going back to work, she said,
even though the boss had told him to take as much time
as he wanted.

'I don't see how he can do his job properly,' she said.
'But he says they really have too much work on for him
to take any time off.'

'Perhaps he needs to be occupied,' I said.

'I don't like the drinking.'

'Maybe not, but – well, perhaps he needs that, too.'
Jodie's mother sighed.

'I expect you're right, dear. He's a sensible sort of chap

really and I suppose we all have to face grief in our own way. I'm going to make him a steak-and-kidney pie tonight to see if I can tempt him.'

'That sounds good,' I said, thinking that maybe looking after Tom was Mrs Bailey's own way of facing grief.

'But, dear,' she went on as we sipped our coffee and Jamie sat at the table and drank his orange juice, 'tell me how you're getting on. You must be finding it hard to manage. Why don't you apply for Jodie's job?'

'You're the second person who's suggested it.'

'It's very handy for you, isn't it?'

'You wouldn't mind? Tom wouldn't be hurt?'

'For heaven's sake, why should he be? Someone will do it. It might as well be you.'

'I know. It's just—'

She leaned forward and put her hand on my arm.

'I know how you feel,' she said. 'How we all feel. I still can't believe—' For a moment she paused, overcome, then she carried on. 'Believe me, dear, Jodie wouldn't mind.'

I'd definitely talk to Mary that very afternoon, I decided, and once Jamie had had his rest I took him over to the farm, much to his and William's delight. They disappeared into the playroom and could be heard pushing cars around with suitable *vroom-vroom* noises accompanied by much shrieking.

Mary agreed enthusiastically that I should apply for Jodie's job, and told me that she had definitely decided to go back to work herself. She had trained as a physiotherapist and was not only greatly needed at the hospital but loved the work. And the money wouldn't come amiss, either. Even Roger agreed with that, though he'd been dubious about the wisdom of leaving Jess at first.

'I can't say I like that aspect much myself,' Mary said.

'But I spoke to Grace Polmear today and she's really anxious to do the job and doesn't want a fortune for it. She just loves being with children, she said. Having her would be like having an extra grandma, wouldn't it? We all know her so well, she's practically a member of the family already. And it'll be wonderful if we can share the cost. Roger will be all for that!'

'I haven't got the job yet!'

'Oh, I do hope you manage it,' Mary said. 'It'll be a real new beginning for you. Did you say anything to Ian about it last night?'

'He suggested it, actually.' I was aware of a sudden and quite irrational wave of irritation at the very thought of a third party organising my life, however well meant. Who the hell did Ian Channing think he was? 'He's a great little planner,' I said.

Mary laughed. 'Always was. Don't be cross. He only has your best interests at heart.'

'I know that,' I said, softening a little.

'Why don't you ring them right now? You can at least let them know you're interested.'

'Shall I?' I made up my mind suddenly. 'OK, I will. I've got nothing to lose.'

'And an awful lot to gain.'

I was passed, after a long wait, from a receptionist to Mr Ransleigh, who said he had already interviewed two applicants for the job but hadn't yet made up his mind about either of them. Would I go and see him the following day? Rashly I agreed to do so, banking on Mary being able to have Jamie for an hour or so. I wasn't disappointed. She'd be glad to, she said. And did I want to borrow anything to wear at the interview? There was that cinnamon-coloured jacket that would look wonderful with my black skirt and sweater, particularly if I also borrowed the scarf her mother had sent for her last birthday, which matched the jacket perfectly.

Thus accoutred, with hair newly washed and shoes polished, I set out for Boscothey Manor the following day, feeling considerably smarter than I had done for a long time. It occurred to me that moving on, taking a job, having to make the best of myself, would undoubtedly do me the world of good. I'd been a mess, mentally and physically, for far too long.

Jodie had pointed out Paul Ransleigh to me one day in St Venn, so I knew what to expect, though on that occasion he had been wearing jeans and a fisherman's smock. Now he was dressed in his working gear – an immaculate grey suit, cream-coloured shirt and subdued tie. Even so, he somehow managed to give the impression of being a touch theatrical. Maybe it was the grey-blond hair that hung to his collar, or the perma-tan, or the several gold rings he wore. Or it could have been his manner, which verged on the camp. He seemed nice enough, though. But wet. Definitely wet. Jodie had been right about that.

He treated me to a high-flown pep talk, dwelling on Boscothey's charms, the exceptional standard of service that was demanded of those who worked there, the wealth and pedigree of their guests – eventually pausing to drop his rather high-flown manner and say, more conversationally: 'That's all true, of course, but I had to say it anyway. My wife would kill me if I didn't.'

I laughed, a little uncertainly, not knowing quite what to make of him.

'Well now,' he went on. 'It's your turn. Can you tell me what *you* think you can offer to Boscothey Manor?'

'Well—' My mind seemed to have gone a complete blank, but I swallowed hard and took a deep breath. 'Commitment,' I said. 'I've known Boscothey all my life, in all its phases, and I've always loved it. Loved

the whole area, in fact. I've worked as a secretary
before—'

'You have references?'

'Yes. I have.' One, anyway, from the estate agency,
which he seemed to find satisfactory.

'And of course, you're IT literate? Which is,' he added,
'more than I am.'

'Of course,' I lied, smiling. Well, it was only half a lie.
I was rusty, as Ian had said, but I felt sure it would all
come back to me. Like riding a bicycle, you didn't really
forget it, and even if it was hard at first, it didn't matter
too much. If Paul himself knew little about computers
and all their works, then it was highly likely I would be
able to busk it.

I became aware suddenly that I wanted this job more
than anything. It wasn't only the dressing up and the
application of make-up that made me feel good; it was
the feeling of confidence, the assurance that I could cope,
come what may. I liked it, and I liked the salary the job
paid, which was more than I expected. I took great care
to hide this however.

Mrs Ransleigh shimmied in halfway through the interview. She was middle-aged, but very blonde and very
glitzy, with heavy gold earrings and equally heavy make-
up. Years ago, Jodie had told me, Delia Ransleigh had
been a model and though she'd put on quite a bit of weight
since those days, she was still a striking woman with, I
couldn't help noticing, fantastic legs and very expensive
shoes. I didn't, however, care much for her rather strident,
assertive manner. I couldn't help noticing that the moment
she addressed her husband, he seemed diminished somehow, shrivelling a little and becoming even wetter than
before.

Perched on the edge of the desk, she took over the
interview and gave me the same pep talk all over again.

Then she took me on a tour of the hotel, only it wasn't like other hotels, she insisted, and I was to think of it as a country home, a retreat for those who were only used to the very best. It was the kind of gracious home, she added, that she and Paul had always been used to and they took great delight in sharing it with other appreciative guests. At a price, of course. If I had been a little taken aback by the salary offered, a casual glance at the room rates nearly made my eyes pop out. I didn't know anyone who had that kind of money to spare, barring royalty, pop idols and football heroes.

There was nothing so vulgar as a reception desk, just a gilded *escritoire* tucked away in a discreet nook off the square hall, itself furnished only with a few items, either antiques or reproductions, I was in no position to say which. There were masses of flowers, artistically arranged, and great swags of crimson and gold curtains. A few huge pictures of the family-portrait variety hung on the walls, and at the far end a glorious fireplace – surely the original? – held a log fire that looked, at this moment, as if it could do with a lackey to build it up a little.

The lounge was less dramatic, more *Homes and Gardens*, with another log fire, acres of pastel colours and pale chintz, more flowers, more porcelain, more pictures and a huge selection of glossy magazines on still glossier tables.

'Lovely,' I murmured. And it was, if you liked that sort of thing. I was more of the minimalist persuasion myself.

Up the beautifully restored staircase, the atmosphere of unbridled luxury continued. The rooms were named, not numbered, the doors in the corridor each bearing an exquisite painting of a flower. The Bluebell Room was next to the Primrose Room, the Rose Suite just across the corridor.

31

'This one is empty at the moment,' Delia said, flinging open the door of the Rose Suite. I stood on the threshold and marvelled. It ran almost the length of the house and was the last word in elegance and luxury, all in shades of pink, from the deepest rose to the palest off-white. 'Don't, please, mention it in the village,' Delia went on, 'but we have Sir Paul McCartney and his wife arriving tomorrow for a couple of nights. They want complete privacy and rest – which, of course, brings me to the most important qualification of all, if we are to employ you here. Discretion. Can we rely on you never to speak about our guests away from the hotel?'

'Of course.' I was a little on my dignity. 'If that's part of the job, then I'll honour it.'

'I hope so.'

I wasn't sure if she sounded convinced, but she needn't have worried. Jodie and I might have gossiped with the best about people we knew, but, now I came to think of it, she had never once mentioned anyone who stayed at the hotel and I felt sure I would be able to do the same.

'My father was an officer in the Royal Navy,' I added, as this proved my reliability beyond doubt.

Delia smiled in acknowledgement of this information, though I wasn't at all sure she followed my line of thought. She ushered me out of the Rose Suite and along the corridor, where a further staircase led to more rooms.

I'd only gone a few steps when I stopped and pointed to a small picture on the wall.

'Oh, look,' I said. 'That's a Bagley, isn't it?'

I was showing off, just a bit. Kit always said I belonged to the I-don't-know-anything-about-art-but-I-know-what-I-like school, but I did recognise a Bagley when I saw one because my grandmother had been at school with Ira Bagley's sister. Apparently he had been rather sweet on her at one time and had presented her with two little seascapes which were, even as we spoke, hanging in my cottage. I could have raised quite a bit of money on them and had indeed been tempted, but had decided to keep them, partly as a kind of insurance and partly because I liked them. They were, it seemed, already paying off, though not in the way I might have expected, for Mrs Ransleigh favoured me with a smile which was noticeably less condescending than before.

'My dear, how clever of you,' she said, surprised. 'It's not everyone who's even heard of him, though he's enjoying a vogue at the moment.'

'I think they're lovely,' I said. 'No one paints the sea quite like he does. I have two small paintings of his at home.'

'Really?' For some reason this seemed to impress her. 'I agree with you, his paintings are quite unique.'

'He was a friend of my grandmother's,' I said.

'Really?'

This, too, seemed to find favour, as if some of Bagley's glory must have transferred itself to me, resulting in her manner becoming considerably warmer. She even went so far as to say how nice it would be to have someone of culture and taste joining the staff. I suppressed my amusement, delighted that the job appeared to be mine and at the same time hoping that she wasn't inspired to question me about any other art treasures. This, I was only too aware, would undoubtedly reveal my almost total ignorance of such things.

The tour continued, but to my relief I was not called to do more than utter appreciative exclamations. It was, indeed, all very beautiful, and the few guests I came across in the corridors and public rooms seemed universally pleasant, well dressed and unmistakably wealthy.

'Of course, we have a marvellous staff,' Delia Ransleigh said as we descended the wide staircase together. 'Mrs Willis, the housekeeper, is quite wonderful. I'm nominally in charge of that side of the operation and she reports to me, as do Carol and Isobel, the two receptionists. Paul is in charge of the finances and the general organisation. Our chef, Gaston, is straight from Paris. He's our biggest asset, I always say. You'll be meeting the whole team, of course, when you join us.'

'So you're offering me the job?'

'Er . . .' she hesitated a moment. 'It's Paul's decision really, but yes, I think you can take that for granted. We'll put a letter in the post, of course, dotting the i's and crossing the t's, but if you could possibly start on Monday . . .?'

I panicked like mad when I got back to Mary.

'I must be crazy,' I said. 'I had no idea what the place was like. I know Jodie said it was luxurious, but I didn't know the half of it. I'm bound to make a hash of it.'

'Rubbish,' Mary said as she handed me a restorative cup of tea. 'What difference does luxury make? More to the point, did they show you the office equipment?'

'Briefly. I think I can cope.'

'Of course you can cope!'

'Apparently they only really get busy after Easter.'

'That'll give you a few weeks to work yourself in.'

'And Monday will be all right? If Grace isn't here by then, I got the impression that a few days more wouldn't matter too much.'

'Grace will be here. I'll be here too, until Wednesday, just to give her time to find out the routine and learn where everything's kept. It's all working out wonderfully,

Prue, so stop worrying. This is the beginning of the next phase and you're going to be brilliant.'

She sounded convinced. I sighed, and smiled, trying to feel the same. Convinced or not, I was moving on, and the thought excited me.

Three

I was nervous when I presented myself for work that first morning, but I think I managed to put a fairly good face on it. Paul was welcoming and did his best to put me at ease by taking me on a tour of the kitchen and introducing me to the rest of the staff. I revised my opinion of him a little. I still thought he was a bit wet, but in a nice, gentle, self-mocking sort of way that made me think we would get along quite well together, in spite of the perma-tan. It was notice-able, however, that it was Delia who ruled the roost, and from the start I was wary of her. I could tell she was not one to overlook any mistakes, on my part or anyone else's.

We had completed the tour and were back in the office when she breezed in, gave a quick greeting, and rushed off again to some meeting in St Venn connected with the tourist board. I had the distinct feeling that for the whole of this brief episode Paul was holding his breath, as if expecting some form of reproof or a disparaging comment. Once she had left, he visibly relaxed, and I wondered what, if anything, he had to hide. Or perhaps he was so used to his wife finding fault with him that he expected it, whether he deserved it or not.

'Now for the general routine,' he said, getting down to explaining my duties. It appeared there was a standard formatted reply for routine letters, but that he liked to dictate when more complicated matters were involved. 'How's your shorthand?' he asked.

'Fine,' I said. This, like the claim to computer skills, was only half a lie. I'd been fairly speedy in my previous office days, but once again I was rusty. I could only hope that it would all come back to me once I was put to the test.

'We're reasonably quiet until Easter,' Paul went on. 'After that, things hot up considerably. Including the marriage business, of course. We started that last year, as you possibly know. Only the more exclusive ones – the price sees to that! It's a lucrative business, but it means there's more correspondence to deal with, and it will be your job to make sure that everything ties in – church, flowers, photographers and so on. Mind you, I'm finding out that every bride has her own ideas about how things should be done, not to mention the bride's mother, who probably has a complete set of utterly different ones. Tact, it seems, is often called for – but then, when isn't it in this business? Obviously we have to get things absolutely right – the bride's big day and all that, never mind the marriage probably won't last a year. Jodie was brilliant at all of this.' He shuffled some papers and cleared his throat, as if he found it painful to think of her.

'I'm sure she was,' I murmured, wondering if I was ever going to be able to fill her shoes.

'Then there's the office diary,' Paul went on. 'It's up to you to enter all my appointments – and Delia's, too. It's here, on this table, and it's absolutely essential that it's kept up to date. I warn you, my memory's hardly the best in the west, and I'm afraid it's your job to see I don't forget appointments or double-book things. And when any VIP is due, the receptionist of the day will let you know the time of arrival, and this must be recorded too, because it's hotel policy for either Delia or me to greet them personally. A little red-carpet treatment goes an awfully long way, we find.'

'I'll do my best,' I said, but I must have sounded doubtful, for he smiled at me reassuringly.

'You'll soon get the hang of it. Jodie used to stick Post-it notes all over my desk. Delia didn't like it but I never minded. For me, everything has to be written down, or I'm lost. I shall rely on you to keep me on the straight and narrow.'

My fears, which had been starting to subside a little, stirred once more into life. It seemed to me that I was being relied on for a lot of things that were likely to be outside my control, including Paul Ransleigh's uncertain memory.

But there was no time to worry about that. Paul was continuing to enumerate my duties: the changing menus that had to be set out and printed off, the cash book where I was to enter the deposit paid by any guest who wanted to hire the hotel's boat, *Firefly*. He showed me the little cabinet on the wall close to my desk which held the keys, together with duplicate keys of all the hotel vehicles.

'Only to be used in an emergency,' he said. 'Don't let any member of staff think he can breeze in and borrow a car whenever he feels like it. Or she,' he added. 'It's Isobel you have to watch, to be honest. If she wants a car at any time, make sure you check with me first. She's a lousy driver.'

I smiled weakly. Isobel was a woman in her mid-forties, well groomed and highly enamelled, with a wide smile she was very ready to bestow on Paul – but not, I quickly discovered, upon his new secretary. I had the distinct impression that she wanted to impress her seniority and superior knowledge on me from the first; it was clear in her body language and her offhand acknowledgement of my existence. Oh well, I thought, you can't win 'em all.

We had left her and continued on our way, with Paul still issuing instructions. 'You can go to the kitchen at midday to get something to eat,' he said. 'Or for coffee at more or less any time. Don't be put off by Gaston. He can be an irascible old devil but his bark's worse than his bite. Strictly between you and me, I think he's rather susceptible to pretty young women, so you'll probably have him eating out of your hand.'

I hoped he would eventually prove to be right, for my first impressions had seemed to say something quite different. Gaston was a short man with a huge stomach, wild eyes and black hair that stood out in every direction around his tall hat. He was clearly going through some kind of crisis – caused by halibut, I soon discovered, which hadn't arrived when it should have done – involving a great deal of gesticulation, clattering of pots and swearing, in several languages. Seldom had I felt more instinctively terrified of anyone, and was definitely unable to discern any sign of susceptibility to me or anyone else. It was clear he ruled the kitchen with a rod of iron and I very much hoped he improved upon acquaintance. As it was, he barely appeared to notice my presence and it was left to the young sous-chef, Sean Beaumont, to do the honours.

He was a very different kettle of *poisson*, as Gaston might have said, being tall and dark and quite staggeringly handsome, dark hair curling around his ears and his hat, spectacular blue eyes with fabulous lashes and a devastating smile, all this allied to a faint Irish brogue. He had, as my mother said of Kit, a way with him, which in itself was enough to make me a touch suspicious; but his charm was warming for all that.

'Be sure to come back at lunchtime,' he said to me. 'I'll make you a prawn sandwich so good you'll swear it floated down from the heavens.'

'Thanks. I'll look forward to it.'

Paul waved his hand around, vaguely indicating a thin,

blonde girl unloading plates from the vast dishwasher and an older woman busy at the sink.

'There we have Mandy and Mrs Clemow – ah, and here's Mrs Willis, who may allow you to call her Marcia if you play your cards right. It's she who keeps the whole show on the road. Marcia, meet Prue. She's come to take poor Jodie's place.'

Mrs Willis was the housekeeper, I remembered. She was a pleasant-faced woman, probably in her late fifties, who smiled and nodded at me.

'You're very welcome,' she said. 'Though we're all sad about the reason you've come. And take no notice of Paul. He thinks flattery will get him anywhere.'

'Not a word of flattery about it,' Paul protested. 'Marcia keeps all the cleaners on the straight and narrow and no speck of dust worth its salt allows itself to be seen. We're all terrified of her.'

'Get along with you,' Marcia said.

The easy, joking relationship between them had the effect of making me feel more at home. Maybe life at Boscothey Manor wasn't entirely full of stress and strain, and there might after all be lighter moments. Maybe it wouldn't be too long before I learned the ropes and became one of the inner circle. I found I was leaving the kitchen in a marginally more confident frame of mind than I entered it.

Thankfully, when Paul later left the office, there were only some routine letters for me to cope with. I found these easy enough, and at lunchtime I put them in his in-tray for signing and went down to the kitchen, as instructed. Sean was as good as his word. He made me the promised prawn sandwich, which was delicious, introduced me to various other members of staff who were now present (two of them I knew already as they were Trenellack women who'd worked as cleaners at the hotel from the day it opened) and chatted to me amusingly while I ate. But even as I laughed at his jokes I looked up to see Mandy, the pretty, pale little kitchen assistant, giving me a look in which misery and loathing seemed equally apportioned. The implication was clear. She appeared to think I was trespassing on her preserve, so I finished my sandwich, thanked Sean for his ministrations and beat a strategic retreat as soon as possible.

I was glad to have a few minutes' breathing space to spend on my own and familiarise myself with my own particular work space.

The office wasn't large, but it held all necessary equipment quite comfortably and had a big sash window overlooking the back courtyard that brought in plenty of light. Facing me across the yard was the kitchen wing, and I found I could see Gaston in his tall hat as he crossed from one end of the room to the other, then Mandy going in the other direction. Not exactly a magnificent panorama, I reflected, but potentially interesting.

I turned my attention to the computer. The work I'd done earlier was too simple to make me feel really conversant with all its functions, so I looked around to see if I could find the manual.

I couldn't, but in the bottom drawer of the desk I found other things that shocked me into immobility for a second or two. Clearly this was the drawer where Jodie had kept a few personal belongings. On the top there were a couple of magazines, a shocking-pink folding umbrella which I had seen in use many times, and a silk scarf, green with a pattern of paler leaves. Slowly I reached to pick it up, and as I lifted it I could smell a faint breath of her favourite perfume. It was enough to send a wave of misery and loss through me once more. For a moment I held it in both hands, then carefully folded it and put it back in the drawer. Oh, why had it happened? Why had she *allowed* it to happen? I felt almost angry with her now. How could she possibly have been so careless when she knew the dangers so well?

'Getting on all right?' a voice asked me, breaking in on my thoughts and causing me to jump a little. It was Delia, tip-tapping into the office on her three-inch heels. Unhurriedly I closed the bottom drawer. For some peculiar and indefinable reason I didn't want to share Jodie's possessions with Delia at that moment. I'd take them to Tom myself.

'Yes. Everything's fine,' I said.

'Paul told you about the diary? And the routine for the VIPs?' It was almost as if she couldn't trust him to do the simplest thing, I thought.

I nodded. 'Yes. He made it all very clear.'

She laughed, amused but with an edge of bitterness.

'Well, there's always a first time, I suppose. I'm only sorry I wasn't able to see to your introduction, but it couldn't be helped. So you think you'll be able to cope?'

'It all seems fairly straightforward so far.'

'Oh, it is. Perfectly simple, really. It's just that Paul can make such a meal of things . . .'

'No, really. Everything's fine.'

She chatted a little more about the class of guests the hotel attracted and the ever-present risk that the wrong kind of person would choose to go there.

'I mean,' she said, 'one doesn't want to be snobbish, but we strive to be exclusive.'

'No footballers' wives?' I asked innocently, tongue in cheek.

'Not if we can help it. Anyway, they would feel quite out of place here. We cater for an entirely different market.'

I waited until she had gone before turning my attention to Jodie's drawer again, lifting out the umbrella, scarf and magazines, wondering why on earth I hadn't mentioned them to Delia. I could have asked her for a plastic bag to carry them in if I hadn't chosen to be so inexplicably secretive about them. It was the perfume, I thought obscurely. For a moment it had brought Jodie so close.

There were a few other things in the drawer – a post-card from someone called Dora from Taormina, saying that the weather was beautiful and she was having a lovely time; and right at the back there was a floppy disk.

What, I wondered as I held it in my hands, was so special about this particular disk? There was no indica-tion of its contents. Was it something personal to Jodie, or was it something to do with the hotel that was out of place and ought to be with all the others in the box on the desk? Or maybe it was music she had recorded, or had borrowed from someone else.

Curious, I slotted it into the computer, brought it up on the screen, and saw at once why Jodie had kept it apart. This, clearly, was a disk that she used for her own private business, accounts and correspondence. There were files for House Insurance, Mortgage, Electricity, Bank, Holiday and so on. How odd, I thought. If I'd given the matter any thought, I would have guessed that it was Tom who held the purse strings and managed all the prac-tical finances – which just shows how little one knows about other people's marriages.

This, I thought as I scrolled idly through, would have to go back to Tom with the other personal things Jodie had left behind. I knew, uneasily, that I probably should-n't be doing this at all. What business was it of mine? Absolutely none, of course, but I didn't imagine Jodie would have minded. I was only looking at the names of the files, not opening any of them, and I found it mildly interesting to see how much of the household accounts

Jodie had apparently controlled. A pity, I thought, that I hadn't been so meticulous when Kit and I were together.

Suddenly I was surprised into stillness. I had come upon a file entitled 'Channing'.

Channing? Ian Channing? Could it possibly be? As far as I was aware, she'd only met him that one time, when we'd all co-operated on the tearing-off of the wallpaper. Why on earth would she be writing to him? And if she had, why hadn't Ian mentioned it?

Yes, I was being nosy. I admit it. But could any woman have prevented curiosity getting the upper hand under these circumstances? If the positions were reversed, Jodie would have done just the same, I had no doubt of that. I clicked on the name and at once a letter came up on the screen. It was dated 2 March.

'Dear Ian,' Jodie had written.

I don't know if you remember me, but we met at Prue's cottage when we were all helping with the redecoration.

I very badly need your help and advice in a professional – well, sort of professional – capacity. I don't know who else to ask. Prue has always spoken highly of you, so I feel you may be the one. Something very worrying indeed has come to my notice and I don't know what to do about it. I'm afraid it may be a serious criminal matter, but I don't really want say more at this moment.

I have tried phoning your office for an appointment, but your secretary says you are very busy and I have no hope of seeing you before Friday, 10 March, which I am afraid will be too late. She also says you're away this coming weekend, otherwise I'd try to contact you privately at home. Believe me, I need to see you urgently and I would be most grateful if you could possibly be kind enough to give me an appointment before next Wednesday, 8 March, at the latest. It really is crucial that

I see you before then. I can make myself free to come to Truro at any time. Please phone me on the above number if you can fit me in.

That was all, apart from 'Yours sincerely'. There was no hint of what this urgent matter might be, why Wednesday was of such importance. Hearing Delia's footsteps approaching the office once more, I instinctively pressed the key to clear the letter from the screen. It might not be any of my business, I thought, but it sure as hell wasn't any of hers either.

She had a long list of jobs for me to do and spent some time telling me where to find various bits of information and going over all the things Paul had told me, as if she still didn't think he had explained enough of the basic office requirements. Against my inclinations, I had to admit to myself that she was a lot more lucid than her husband, who tended to muddy the waters by rambling off in several different directions at once. Certainly I was left in no doubt as to who was the driving force in the running of this hotel, but of the two of them, I found Paul far easier to like.

By the time I'd finished the work she had given me, it was time to go home and I was mightily glad of it. It wasn't that I had worked unduly hard, but the whole day had been a strain, out of practice as I was – and no small part of the strain was caused by my desperate efforts to appear quite sure of myself and my skills. It was a great relief to find that they hadn't been completely forgotten.

Delia seemed to be quite satisfied with my labours, anyway. I finally told her about finding Jodie's scarf and umbrella, though not about the disk. I knew it was one that Jodie had taken from the office cupboard, which might be sufficient reason for Delia to commandeer it, and I didn't imagine that Jodie or Tom would have wanted it to be in her hands, not with all the private information it contained. I told her I was going to take everything to give to Tom.

'Of course, you must have known Jodie,' she said, sounding as if this was a thought that hadn't occurred to her until that moment.

'Yes, we were friends.'

'I hadn't realised.'

'I mentioned it to Paul.'

'Yes . . . well . . .' her voice trailed away, as if anyone would expect that anything told to Paul would be forgotten on the instant.

It was a fact, however, that at my interview I hadn't stressed my life-long friendship with Jodie because of all kinds of mixed-up, ambiguous emotions – partly, I suppose, because I still felt guilty about profiting from Jodie's death, partly because I wanted to get the job entirely on my own merits.

'We were both brought up in Trenellack,' I said, and was about to go on to say that Jodie and I had been best friends since schooldays when I was forestalled by Delia, her voice now throbbing with emotion.

'I liked to think that she and I were particularly close,' she said. I managed to hide my surprise. This was certainly not the impression Jodie had given me. 'So you can imagine how shattered I was – how shattered we all were – when we heard the news. I was quite, quite distraught. Paul and I both felt we had lost someone from our own family, we were so fond of her. And of course, we feel heartsick on her husband's behalf. The poor man! They hadn't been married for very long, hadn't they?'

'Two years.'

'So tragic! Oh, how could she have been so foolhardy as to use that path?'

'I think everyone wonders that.'

'She was in a hurry, of course. Wanted to get home.'
Delia sighed heavily at this reflection on impetuous youth,
her head tilted gravely to one side, her eyes melting with
sorrow. 'Tell me, how is her husband coping?'

'Not too well, I believe.'

'Poor man, poor man!'

'Yes,' I said, feeling instinctively that these were little
more than empty words; in fact I found it rather offen-
sive that she chose to exaggerate her feelings in this way.
And then I felt ashamed, because how was I to know how
she felt? How anyone felt? Maybe she had been as fond
of Jodie as she said, which made it rather sad that Jodie
hadn't realised it.

'It'll be no trouble for me to drop the things in to Tom,'
I said.

'Good. Good.' She smiled at me sweetly. 'Well, so ends
your first day. Off you go – and by the way, do call me
Delia. We're one happy family here, you know.'

Remembering Mandy, the girl in the kitchen who
looked at me with the eyeballs of death, Gaston's temper,
Isobel Baine's chilly acknowledgement of me and Delia's
manner with Paul, I could only hope my smile wasn't too
cynical.

A couple of nights later, Ian dropped in at the cottage.
Despite my assurances to Delia, I hadn't found the time
to take Jodie's belongings to Tom and still had them in
my possession. So far, I was finding that day-to-day living
occupied all my energy. Ensuring that Jamie and I were
fed and had clean clothes to wear seemed to be taking
all my powers of organisation, to the exclusion of everything else.

And really, there didn't appear to be any urgency about
it, though I was curious to know what Ian had made of
the letter Jodie had written to him. I was glad, therefore,
when I saw his white BMW pull up outside the cottage,

though it occurred to me that he would probably tell me nothing, citing client confidentiality, even though this particular client was no longer alive.

When I mentioned it, however, he was completely mystified and denied that he had ever received any form of communication from Jodie.

'I only met her that one time. Why would she be writing to me?'

'Because she was worried and wanted to consult you about something.'

'Like what?'

'She didn't say what it was, exactly. Just that she was desperate to see you before Wednesday of that week. Apparently she'd phoned your secretary, who told her she hadn't a hope of seeing you before Friday.'

'That sounds like our Glenys,' Ian said. 'She does tend to be over-protective.'

'But you never got the letter?'

'No, I didn't. I wonder why she didn't email me?'

'Maybe that would have been too open. Whatever was bothering her, she wasn't giving anything away. It was all a bit cloak-and-dagger.'

'Very odd. I guess she thought better of it and didn't post it after all.'

'Would your Glenys have kept it from you for some reason? Given it to some junior, perhaps?'

'Not if it was specifically addressed to me. It can't have been sent.'

'It sounded so urgent,' I said. I was seeing to Jamie's supper over this exchange, moving about the kitchen from fridge to stove to table and back again. Now I stood, lost in thought, holding a pot of Mr Men strawberry yoghurt just out of his reach.

'*Yog*,' he said ferociously, pointing his spoon at me, his face a mask of tragedy. 'I want it now.'

48

'Don't we all,' Ian said, *sotto voce.*

'Sorry, darling.' I dropped a kiss on the top of Jamie's blond head, recovering myself quickly. 'Concentrate on the letter,' I instructed Ian.

'Why would she consult me?' he asked after a moment.

'Apparently I have spoken highly of you. Can't imagine why,' I added drily.

He picked up a small teddy bear that was on the table beside him and threw it in my direction.

'Must have been a moment's aberration,' he said. 'Well, I suppose I can guess what it was about.'

'You can?' I looked at him in some astonishment. 'Tell me.'

'Well, mostly I handle divorces,' he said. 'Ten to one it was that – or some kind of domestic. If it wasn't, why didn't she tell Tom and ask his advice?'

'Divorce? Jodie and Tom? You're crazy! They were blissfully happy together. Anyway, she said it was a criminal matter and that it was crucial that she saw you before the following Wednesday.'

'And she wrote it when . . .?'

'The 2nd. The previous Thursday.'

'You didn't think to print it out?'

'No, I didn't really have the time. Or the opportunity. Anyway, I thought you'd already seen it, didn't I?'

'I suppose. I wonder what the hell it was about.'

'We'll never know now. She died on Tuesday, the 7th, just five days later.'

Ian was silent for a moment, as I wiped Jamie's mouth and took his plate and mug away to put in the sink.

'Can you remember exactly what she said?' he asked.

I paused and thought about it.

'Just what I've told you,' I said. 'That she was worried about something that could be a criminal matter, and badly needed your advice.'

'And she didn't elaborate on what sort of criminal matter?' he asked. 'She didn't give any clues at all?'

'No. I'll print out the letter, then you can see for yourself. I'll fax it to you, it you like. She sounded quite desperate, Ian. Almost as if – as if . . .' I paused, trying to remember Jodie's exact wording.

'As if what?' Ian prompted.

'As if she was really, really worried. As if she expected something terrible to happen.'

Realising what I had said, I became very still, then slowly turned to look at him in silence. He returned the look, appearing for the first time as if he appreciated the desperation of Jodie's cry for help.

'Well it did, didn't it?' he said at last.

Four

'I think the police ought to know about this,' Ian said.

'If Jodie had wanted the police to know, she would have told them,' I objected.

'And now she can't tell them, even if she wanted to. She's been very effectively silenced.'

'By someone else? Ian, you can't believe—'

'I don't know what I believe! I haven't seen the letter yet. Naturally, like everyone else, I've assumed it to be an accident, but now you tell me she was afraid and worried about something she knew but hadn't mentioned to anyone. Did she fall or was she pushed?'

'I wonder why she didn't post that letter,' I said. 'Why didn't she fax it, if it was urgent, like I intend to?'

Ian said nothing but stared into space, deep in thought. Then he shook his head.

'Look, Prue,' he said. 'Maybe after all we're reading too much into it. The fact that it wasn't sent must tell us something, surely. She could have found out there was nothing to worry about after all and changed her mind about seeing me. And the accident was as it seemed – tragic, but just an accident.'

'Mm.' I thought this over as I took Jamie on to my knee. He was getting sleepy and I'd have to take him for a bath and bed very soon now. 'It's worrying, though. You should see the letter for yourself. Take the disk home and have a look.'

'I will. But whatever it says, maybe Tom could shed light on it.'

'I didn't get the impression she'd discussed it with him.'

This, too, gave Ian pause for thought.

'Well, how about this for a scenario?' he said at last. 'She might have thought he was mixed up in something not quite legal and then found out he wasn't. Or something,' he added, as I looked at him, exasperated.

'That's absolute rubbish, Ian. Tom's totally honest. Everyone knows that.'

Ian smiled – condescendingly, it seemed to me, like a world-weary solicitor who had seen it all.

'My dear girl, I've been too long in the legal game to take the slightest bit of notice of what everyone knows, or thinks they know. All sorts of unlikely people can be capable of all sorts of illegalities.'

'Guilty till proved innocent, is that what you're saying? I had no idea you were so cynical.'

'If you'd seen as much of the dark side of life—'

'Don't be so patronising,' I snapped. 'I've experienced quite a bit of the dark side of life, thank you, but I can still recognise a good man when I see one. And Tom's one of the best.'

I stood up abruptly to carry Jamie towards the steep little flight of stairs that led from the living room. 'And I'm not your dear girl,' I added over my shoulder.

I left him sitting there, looking mildly astonished at my outburst. Maybe I had gone over the top a bit, but I couldn't possibly believe that Tom had done anything to worry Jodie, no matter how many unlikely villains Ian had met in the course of his life.

Jamie was in the bath when I heard his footsteps coming up the stairs.

'Sorry,' he said, leaning against the door-jamb. 'I didn't mean to patronise you and I swear I was just thinking aloud, exploring every angle, not accusing Tom of anything. It's a rotten situation for you, I do realise that. But I still think we should show him the letter. If they were as close as you say, then he might well have a clue what she was worried about. And if Jodie was really on to something and put herself in danger because of it, then it's even more necessary to tell him.'

'We?' I had been bent over the bath, concentrating on Jamie, but turned to look at him as he stood in the doorway. 'I don't really see why you should be involved.'

'The letter was addressed to me.'

'You said it yourself, you never received it.'

'Even so . . .' He hesitated a moment. 'Look, just call me curious. I'd like to hear what Tom has to say. Maybe you could ring him and see if Sunday morning is a good time to call round.'

He could, it dawned on me, be quite forceful when he chose. It was a side of him that I hadn't really appreciated before.

I didn't answer him at once, but whooshed a couple of plastic ducks in Jamie's direction, swishing the water about and prompting the gurgles of mirth that this activity always caused. Then, amid protests, I lifted him out of the bath and enfolded him in a towel.

'Well?' Ian prompted.

'Only if you swear you're not suspecting him of anything,' I said. 'Tom's bound to be in a fragile state, so promise to be nice to him.'

'For heaven's sake, of course I'll be nice. What do you take me for?' Ian sounded amused, but I detected a tinge of genuine indignation and I relented a little towards him. He had, after all, been very nice to me over the past few months.

'It'll be good to have you there,' I said, and could see at once from his expression that this admission had pleased him. Careful, I warned myself. Keep your guard up. Don't let him – or anyone – get too close.

We arranged that I should phone Tom to see if midday on Sunday would be a convenient time to return Jodie's belongings.

'They do a pretty good Sunday lunch at the Ship Inn,' Ian said. 'We could go on there afterwards.'

'Jamie will be with us,' I pointed out, not knowing if he'd taken this into account.

'I know that. But it isn't a starchy place and they don't mind children, especially well-behaved ones like Jamie.'

The way to a mother's heart, I thought. Praise her offspring.

'OK, then. I'd enjoy that. Thanks.'

He *was* nice, I couldn't deny it, and he really seemed to enjoy Jamie's company, which was another point in his favour. If I were looking for a permanent commitment, I could do an awful lot worse.

But I wasn't, I wasn't! I shied away from the very idea like a startled fawn. Men and women could be friends, couldn't they? And that's what we were. Good friends.

He reached out and took my small son out of my arms and, hoisting him to his shoulders, jog-trotted him to his tiny bedroom, causing squeals of joy. He seems at home here already, I thought apprehensively. I can't, I mustn't, let it go too far. I can't let it happen again – the closeness and dependence and trust. I was haunted by the memory of how it had felt, being tied to someone whose endearments and loving ways had changed to ill-tempered abuse, all within the space of two short years. How could I ever be sure that it wouldn't happen again? No one could have been more convincing than Kit.

'Please don't over-excite him,' I said stiffly to Ian as I followed them into the room; and felt mean when he turned to look at me, eyebrows raised in comic astonishment.

'Spoilsport,' he said, pulling a face at me. Which, I thought guiltily, was no more than I deserved.

By the end of the week I was beginning to go about my duties at the hotel with a lot more confidence. Isobel Baines remained distant, but Carol, the other reception-ist, made up for it. Though she was considerably older than I, she was a friendly kind of woman with a great sense of humour, and we hit it off immediately. We took to having our coffee breaks together on the days she had the morning shift, and one day she filled me in regard-ing Isobel's background. She'd had a lousy life. Brought up in a children's home, pregnant at fourteen, nothing but unremitting poverty until some far-seeing social worker had recognised her potential and taken her in hand.

'Don't for heaven's sake tell her I told you,' Carol said, 'but you really have to admire Isobel. She pulled herself up by her boot-straps, stopped mixing with druggies, smartened herself up, got a few GCSEs – and now look at her! You couldn't meet anyone more stylish, could you? Or efficient,' she added.

'You couldn't,' I agreed. 'Well, good for her.'

'Of course, Delia doesn't care for her much. But then Delia doesn't care for anyone who doesn't have a huntin', shootin', fishin' background.'

I laughed. 'Well that excludes me, then.'

'Not at all, my dear. We were all informed before you arrived that you came from a very cultured family and that your father had been a high-ranking naval officer. We all assumed you'd been to Roedean at the very least.'

'St Venn Grammar,' I said. 'And very good it was too.'

'It's strange, really,' Carol went on. 'I have a shrewd suspicion that Delia's background is possibly not that far different from Isobel's. Maybe that's why she's so keen to distance herself from it.'

'What does it matter anyway?' I asked, mildly exasperated by it all. 'We are what we are.'

'I agree.' Carol looked at her watch. 'Time we were back at our posts, or what Delia will be is incandescent.'

At lunchtimes Sean, totally ignoring the black looks thrown towards us by Mandy, continued to exert his charm in my direction, and every day I was struck afresh by his startling looks and his air of sophistication. He seemed to have been everywhere – had lived in London, Paris and Rome, he told me, and much preferred cities to country life. He seemed to me the last sort of person one would expect to find in a Cornish kitchen, even the kitchen of a hotel like this one.

Mandy clearly adored him, though it appeared that the mock-flirtation he carried on with her was no more meaningful or more intimate than the way he treated any other woman. He just couldn't seem to help it. It was, I felt, the only way he knew to talk to a female of any age under any circumstances. We were no more than audiences before whom he felt it necessary to display his many attractions, like a peacock spreading his tail.

Mandy was marginally less hostile towards me when she discovered that I had a little boy. She seemed to think that it put me in a different age bracket – out of the running, as it were – and I'm sure it did. Even if Sean's apparent interest in me were something more than the amusement of the moment – which I didn't believe for a second – I knew at once that he was not a man for commitment; to me, to Mandy or to anyone else, but particularly not to anyone carrying my sort of baggage.

I found he was very good at his job. Gaston was parsimonious with his compliments, and he was very jealous of his authority, but though he did his fair share of swearing at Sean, in English and French, he still commended his work. Often Sean was allowed to be independently creative, and as one who was sometimes the beneficiary, I could only agree that he had tremendous flair. I felt certain it wouldn't be long before he moved on to even greater heights.

On the Thursday of my third week, as I was leaving the hotel to go home across the field, I met him coming from the direction of the cliff path. He was dressed in jeans and a thick sweater, which was very different from his usual cook's garb and somehow made him look more rugged, more masculine and even more handsome.

'Hi!' he called out. 'It's a great day.'

'Wonderful,' I called back. And indeed it was – another of those sunny spring days that lifted the spirits.

I waited until he was closer before asking him if the cliff path was repaired yet.

He looked puzzled.

'Repaired? Oh, you mean along there, where Jodie . . .' His voice trailed away as he nodded his head in the direction of the cliff path that led to Trenellack. 'No. I mean, I don't know. I didn't go that far, only as far as the beach.'

'Right. Well, see you tomorrow . . .' I made as if to go on my way, up the path across the valley field, but he fell in beside me.

'I'll walk with you – if you don't mind, that is?'

'Not a bit.'

'I need the exercise and I can't walk down that way yet,' he said, jerking his head once more in the direction of the cliff path. I glanced at him and saw that his expression was unusually sombre. 'I was very fond of Jodie, you know. She was a great girl.'

'She was,' I agreed.

'I gather from the chat in the kitchen that you and she were good friends, just as we were. I expect she told you.'

'No, she didn't mention you.' He was so pleased with

himself that I confess it gave me a small and totally unworthy *frisson* of satisfaction to say it. 'Actually, she didn't talk about the hotel much at all,' I went on, relenting a little. 'Paul told me right from the beginning it was necessary to be discreet, and she certainly took that to extremes. As far as Boscothey was concerned, Trappist monks had nothing on her.'

'Really?' Sean's serious mood seemed to have passed and he flashed his usual smile at me. 'Then she was unique among women. I thought you all enjoyed nothing more than a good gossip.'

I smiled sweetly at him.

'Maybe she didn't think there was anyone worth gossiping about here.'

'Ouch! Why so prickly?'

I decided that a small amount of teasing wouldn't come amiss.

'I'm not really. You've been kind to me, and I'm grateful. Still, you've got to admit that you consider yourself God's gift to womankind.'

He grinned again, unoffended.

'Sure, and why not? It passes the time in this dead-and-alive hole. What else is there to do, at all?'

I thought of pointing out that this was hardly fair on Mandy, who clearly laboured under the impression that he was her property, but I dismissed the idea. For one thing it sounded impossibly old-maidish, and for another it wouldn't have done the slightest bit of good.

'I must say I find plenty to do,' I said. 'More than plenty, now I'm working. But then I do have a little boy.'

'What do you do for fun?' he asked, stopping in his tracks and swinging me round, his hands on my shoulders.

'Fun?' I must have sounded as if I had no notion of the word's meaning.

'Fun,' he repeated. 'You know, that thing that involves going out, having a good time, going to parties. Look, come out to dinner with me. I've discovered a great little fish restaurant in St Venn. Let me introduce you to it before it gets famous and you have to book two years ahead to get a table.'

'I don't think I can—'

'Sure, you could if you wanted to.'

'I have to find a babysitter—'

'Now don't be telling me you couldn't do that if you tried.'

Could I? Half of me didn't want to be bothered; the other half was thinking how long it was since I'd eaten in a good restaurant with a handsome, amusing man – and maybe I could resurrect that rather nice skirt I'd worn for Jodie's wedding, which would go rather well with the black strappy top that dated from before Jamie was born . . .

'When were you thinking of?' I said weakly.

'I'm off tonight. Come on now – you'd be doing me a favour. Saving me from a lonely evening. Call it an educational trip. I shall be showing you how good food ought to be presented.'

'I can't afford—'

'For heaven's sake, when I ask a girl out, I do the paying. Anyway, I'm pretty friendly with the owners. They do me a special rate.'

'What about Mandy?'

'What *about* Mandy? We're hardly joined at the hip. Anyway, she won't care.'

'No?' I found that rather hard to believe.

'No. She knows you're a mate. And she's on duty.'

'It's rather short notice.'

'I know. I apologise. Isn't there anybody who'd babysit?'

'I'd have to make a few phone calls.'
'You do that,' he said. 'And I'll phone you later.'

Which is how I came to be sitting in the Lobster Pot with Sean later that evening, sipping what he described as a classy Chilean Syrah, about to tuck into my monkfish *à la maison* which, Sean assured me, was prepared in such a way that I'd never be able to bring myself to eat it in any other. Monkfish in *any* way, I assured him, didn't figure largely on my normal menu. At which he laughed and raised his glass in my direction.

'Here's to a gastronomic treat,' he said. 'And better times in future.'

The food was, indeed, wonderful, and clearly Sean and the restaurant's owners had struck up a friendship, for there was much banter between them, which all added to the enjoyment and novelty value for me. It hadn't been easy to find a babysitter, but I was glad now that I had made the effort. I'd pressed into service the teenage son of the family who lived in another cottage similar to mine along the coast road. Jamie knew him and I trusted him; when I finally managed to track him down he said he would welcome the chance to do his homework in peace without his brother and sister around.

'Glad you came?' Sean asked me when at last we had cleared our plates.

'Yes. The food's terrific, I agree.'

'And the company?'

I pretended to consider the question for a moment or two.

'Congenial,' I said at last.

'That's nice. I'm glad you came, too. Tell me, what do you normally do for kicks around here, Prue? God knows I've been in some dull-as-ditchwater places in my time, but – this restaurant excepted, of course – I fail to see why people come here for their holidays. What do they do with themselves, for the love of God?'

I looked at him incredulously.

'But Sean, it's beautiful here,' I said. 'They come to enjoy the scenery and find peace and – and to walk and to recharge their batteries.'

'Sure, sure. But there's plenty of peace when you're six feet down – and on the subject of batteries, mine are in danger of running down altogether. Believe me, I've walked over the entire area, seen all there is to see, sampled the so-called nightlife in St Venn on my evening off. To say I'm underwhelmed doesn't go within an inch of it. Playing bar billiards at the Lugger doesn't exactly thrill me, and unfortunately I can't afford to come to this place all the time. Come on now, tell me: where do all the parties go on in this neck of the woods?'

'Parties?' I laughed at him. 'Well, I'm sure they exist, but I don't have time for much in that line myself.'

'Because of your little boy? Where's his dad? Somewhere local?'

'No. Well—' I corrected myself. 'To be strictly honest, I don't know exactly where he is. He decided that marriage and fatherhood weren't for him, and just kind of melted away.'

'Did he now? Well, maybe he felt like me, that Trenellack wasn't the place for him.'

'Maybe,' I agreed. I didn't want to talk about Kit. Even thinking about him was enough to ruin a perfectly good evening. 'Tell me about you,' I said as, having polished off our crème brûlées, we sat over coffee. 'If you hate the country so much, what are you doing here?'

'Isn't it obvious? I'm learning my trade. From a master. Gaston's one of the top chefs, you know. If he hadn't been guilty of a small indiscretion somewhere along the line, he'd have a raft of Michelin stars by this time.'

'What small indiscretion?'

For a moment he hesitated. Then he shrugged.

'I think that's between him and the French Sureté,' he said. 'Whatever it was, he's paid for it. France's loss is our gain – especially the Ransleighs' and maybe even more especially mine. I propose to learn every damned thing he can teach me before we part company. It's unusual to find a chef like him this far from London or Paris. The hotel wouldn't last five minutes without him.'

'In spite of the luxury and the fabulous setting?'

Sean grinned at me, a cynical gleam in his eye that told me exactly what he thought of both.

'Sure the Ransleighs would be like chickens with their heads chopped off without Gaston,' he said. 'Or Marcia, come to that. They'd be chasing around in all directions, not knowing what to do with the place. Paul's an effete Hooray Henry and Delia is no more than jumped-up trailer-trash, no class at all. She doesn't think the guests see through her, but I can assure you they do.'

I was startled and rather shocked by this. I didn't hold much of a brief for Delia myself, but Sean seemed to be exhibiting a particularly mean streak I hadn't suspected. To Delia's face he was his usual charming, slightly flirtatious self; it struck a discordant note to find him so vitriolic in private. Where was the smooth-tongued charmer now?

'That's not a very nice thing to say!'

He shrugged his shoulders.

'So what? It's all true. A hotel like Boscothey stands or falls by its cuisine.' He picked up his coffee cup and sipped in silence for a moment, his eyes on my face, as if it amused him to see how he had shocked my conventional soul. 'You know something, Prue?' he went on. 'One of these days I'll be famous, and Gaston – yes, and Paul and Delia too – will boast that I once worked for them. I'm not staying down in this God-forsaken hole any longer than I have to, believe me. I want my own place, my own Michelin star.'

'No doubt you'll get them,' I said.

'You better believe it.' He wasn't smiling now, and I could sense the steely determination. 'My own place,' he said again, very softly. 'In London. Patronised by the *crème de la crème*. Columns written about me in the broadsheets and all the glossy magazines. Mark my words, Prue, it'll happen. I dream about it all the time.'

He meant it. No one looking at him now could doubt it. The ruthlessness, the greediness for acclaim showed itself in the thinning of his mouth and the way his face seemed to have sharpened. It was clear to me that I didn't really know him at all.

'Well, I wouldn't mind doing a little bit of boasting myself,' I said, keeping it light. 'So I hope you're right.'

His expression relaxed and he smiled at me, leaning closer and reaching across the table to put his hand on mine. When he spoke, his voice was low, the seductive charm once more on display.

'Sure you're a lovely girl, Prue,' he said. 'Why any man would leave you, I can't imagine.'

I didn't answer. I wasn't exactly a Victorian miss, shocked by a little bit of hand-holding, but I was aware, suddenly, of warning bells. Had I given him the wrong signals? I didn't think so. I certainly hadn't intended to. This was supposed to be a meeting between a couple of friends and colleagues – or so I had thought.

My God, I'm naïve, I thought to myself. Totally out of practice, that was my trouble. What an idiot! I hadn't been able to see beyond the novelty of dressing up and going to eat in a first-class restaurant.

Carefully, casually, I removed my hand on the pretext of picking up the table napkin to dab at my lips.

'Would you tell me something, Sean?' I said.

'Sure.'

'Does Mandy fit into any of your plans and dreams?'

He sat back in his chair with a bark of laughter.

'Mandy? What is all this about Mandy? You seem to be obsessed! Oh, she's quite a sweet kid, I'll give you that, but thick as two short planks.' He laughed again. 'Sure I never heard such a crazy notion. She's not my type at all.'

'Maybe I misunderstood the signs,' I said.

I knew I hadn't though, for Mandy, by this time, had given me several broad hints concerning Sean. I felt angry on her behalf. They both had rooms in the staff block over the old stables, and Mandy had hinted at a number of romantic interludes which she had clearly taken far too seriously. What fools we women made of ourselves whenever a good-looking charmer hove into sight.

'Forget her,' he said.

'Well, let her down gently.'

He was right, of course. Mandy, palely pretty though she was, was a country girl born and bred, under-educated and untravelled. And not – even her best friend would agree – the brightest thing on two legs. I had to admit that it was impossible to imagine her having a place in the kind of world Sean wanted for himself.

He, on the other hand, was set apart from normal mortals, by his looks if by nothing else. I was curious about his upbringing, and asked him about it – more to keep his attention away from me than anything else.

He'd lived much of his life in Paris and was completely bilingual, he told me. His mother was French and worked for a famous fashion designer – had always worked and had kept the family together, for his Irish father had been a wastrel and a gambler. But because he was the younger son of a lord, enough money had somehow been found from the family estate to send Sean, the only son, back to public school in England. All the Beaumonts, for generations, had been educated at Winchester, so that's where his grandfather insisted that Sean should go. Thereafter, he added casually, his holidays had mostly been spent at his grandfather's ancient castle in Tipperary, though sometimes he went to Paris or Rome or wherever his mother happened to be working.

'Which I much preferred, I can tell you,' he went on with an amused twist of his lips. 'I hated the country and escaped to Dublin whenever I could – now there's a city where you can find a good party any night of the week.'

'So where did the cooking come in?'

He shrugged his shoulders.

'I don't know. Guess I always loved it, but it took me a while to realise how much. My grandfather wanted me to stay in Tipperary and run the estate. Or alternatively go in for medicine, or maybe the law. Something worthy, anyway.' He laughed again. 'Can you imagine it? Me, a pillar of the establishment? I chose to bum around the world for a bit. Signed on as part of the crew on a millionaire's yacht in the Caribbean. Jumped ship in the Bahamas and managed to hitch a lift in a private plane to New York. Worked my way across the States – got thrown into prison in San Francisco for getting mixed up in a fight, and so on, and so on. Wonderful years. Of course, I managed to get myself cut off without a penny, but then by the time my grandfather died there weren't many pennies around anyway. I ended up in Paris, where my mother made me go and work in a friend's restaurant. The rest is history. I took to it like a duck to water. So here I am, educated, ambitious, but without a bean.'

The world he described seemed so remote from anything I had ever known that my first reaction was that he was probably having me on; it wouldn't be the first time he'd tested my gullibility and found much amusement in doing so. But then I thought, Why not? The whole story seemed to explain him: his self-possession and air of sophistication. Even his good manners. After all, someone had to be the younger son of a lord. Why not Sean's father?

'I must go,' I said, looking at my watch. 'I promised the babysitter.'

'How's she getting home?'

'It's a he. And he came on his bike.'

'No reason, then, why you can't invite me in for a cup of coffee.'

I drew a long breath.

'Every reason, Sean. I've had a great time, but we both know that's all there is to it.'

He looked at me for a long moment, not smiling any more, but he said nothing, concentrating on paying the bill and helping me into my coat.

I sensed that the evening had gone a little sour and I wondered what he had expected. I didn't feel guilty. I felt I'd made the nature of this date absolutely clear and all I wanted now was to be home, with the door locked against all intruders. We walked to the car in silence and he opened the door for me, like the perfect gentleman he had been brought up to be.

'It really was a lovely dinner, Sean,' I said when we were both inside. 'Thanks again.'

Still silent, he slid an arm around my shoulders and pulled me towards him, his lips clamping on mine before I had time to know what was happening. I twisted my head and pushed him away.

'Don't, Sean,' I said. 'Please don't. You knew I wasn't up for that. Just take me home.'

He sat for a second, holding the wheel, looking straight ahead. Then he gave a short laugh.

'You're a frigid little cow, aren't you? No wonder your husband left you.'

My temper flared. 'I *hate* your sort of man,' I said furiously. 'Because I don't fancy you, then I'm frigid, right? Oh, forget it!' I settled back in my seat again. 'Just take me home.'

'Whatever Madam wishes,' he said through gritted teeth, and started the car.

We were out of town and driving along the coastal road when he spoke again.

'Is it Mandy?' he said. 'Is that what's bothering you? Because, believe me, she doesn't mean a thing to me.'

'It's not Mandy, though I think you're behaving like a complete shit towards her. I'm just not—' I hesitated. 'I'm not ready for anyone – and what's more, I'll never, ever, be ready for anyone like you, so the sooner you get the message the better I'll be pleased.'

He said no more and neither did I. Instead I sat and fumed, thinking how awkward this was going to make everything, and what a fool I had been to accept his invitation in the first place.

'Look,' I said at last. 'Don't let's fall out over this, because we have to work together and so far it's been fun. We both – misinterpreted the situation. Let's leave it at that.'

He stayed silent, not speaking again until we pulled up outside the cottage.

'You're not the girl your friend Jodie was,' he said.

I'd unbuckled the seatbelt preparatory to making a quick getaway, but I paused at this.

'What do you mean?'

'Jodie didn't push me away as if I were something the cat dragged in. We were close, Jodie and I. I told you. She's a great loss.'

'I know,' I said. Adding: 'How close?'

He laughed softly in the darkness and, leaning towards me, ran a finger down the side of my cheek.

'Let's just say she was kinder than you. Had a more giving nature. And man, could she give!'

I looked at him for a moment. There was a three-quarters moon that night and his face glimmered pale in the semi-darkness.

'Jodie loved Tom,' I said. 'She wouldn't have looked at you.'

He laughed again.

'Wouldn't she?' he said. 'Wouldn't she?'

I didn't rise to this.

'Goodnight, Sean,' I said. I got out of the car, slamming the door behind me. Once in bed I couldn't sleep, but lay turning over and over in my mind Sean's implications regarding Jodie. Was he trying to say that they had had an affair? What other interpretation could there be?

I didn't believe it. But it was odd that Jodie had never mentioned him. She had been discreet where the hotel was concerned, that was true, but she'd talked a bit about Paul and Delia and some of the others. Sean's looks were so spectacular that I would have expected her to make some comment about them, however light. Surely she would have done, if friendship had been all that was between them?

But she wouldn't have been unfaithful. I *couldn't* believe it, knowing her and knowing Tom as I did. Sean only said what he did because he wanted to hit back at me – perhaps make me question the quality of the friendship that had existed between us. He knew how hard her death had hit me. And I knew he had a mean streak; his remarks about Paul and Delia and the way he treated Mandy proved that.

Jodie would have chatted with him and laughed with

him, as I did – maybe even flirted with him a little, as I had done but never would again. That would have been all.

But Ian was a divorce lawyer and she had written to him . . .

So what? I asked myself. Did I really think that Jodie was having a serious affair with Sean and was afraid of Tom? The whole idea was utter nonsense. For one thing, Sean wasn't the sort of man to be serious about any woman; and for another, the letter had referred to some kind of criminal activity. And an affair, while it might be deplored, was hardly criminal.

Should I tell Ian what Sean had said? Or would it just muddy the waters? If so much of a whisper of this got to Tom, he wouldn't be able to cope . . .

It was a rotten night.

Five

I was diffident about ringing Tom to arrange the visit Ian had suggested; though I had written a heartfelt letter of condolence to him, I hadn't actually spoken to him since Jodie's death. He sounded subdued and unlike himself when I rang, but made an obvious effort to be friendly and said he would be glad to see us on Sunday. His mother-in-law had gone home to Truro, he said, but would be back for the funeral on Tuesday.

'Oh, and by the way,' he added, 'the inquest has confirmed that it was accidental death. It was just a formality, of course. No one expected anything else.'

Would he still think that when he had seen the letter Jodie had written?

'Well, I'm glad that's over for you, Tom,' I said. 'I wouldn't be bothering you on Sunday except to hand over a few of Jodie's possessions that were at the hotel.'

He sounded more like himself when he answered me.

'It's no bother, Prue. I'll be glad to see you.'

'I'll be with Ian. You met him—'

'I remember,' Tom said, cutting me off. I guessed it was still too painful to think about times like that carefree afternoon when the four of us had scraped old paper off the walls while we sang songs of our youth and laughed at corny jokes.

'Give me a run-down on him,' Ian said to me as we drove towards Trenellack on Sunday morning. 'I know you think he's a great guy, but what really makes him tick?'

We'd borrowed Mary's Metro for the occasion because it had a baby seat in the back, and our conversation was held against the background of Jamie droning his version of 'The Grand Old Duke of York', recognisable only to a fond mother. There had been no opportunity to tell Ian about what Sean had said a couple of evenings before – and even if there had been, I still wasn't sure it was something I wanted to mention.

'You met him,' I said.

'I know, but it was hardly an in-depth encounter, was it?'

'What makes him tick?' I considered the question. 'Jodie. His job. Sailing. They were both pretty gung-ho about outdoor activities – climbing and skiing and so on. They always took those sort of holidays. I remember Tom saying he could take a tropical beach for a day, but after that he was bored stiff.'

'You said this was his second marriage?'

'That's right. I never met his first wife. It all happened in London and was over by the time he came back here.'

'Who left whom?'

'I don't think it was like that. Apparently it was a disaster from the beginning and they both decided to call it a day. I'm sure he gave it his best shot, though. He really is one of the good guys, Ian: good at his job, straight as a die – and he can also be very funny. He was that afternoon, remember? He has a serious side too, of course. He gets worked up about politics and politicians.'

'Don't we all?'

'Maybe, but he seems to take things so personally.'

'Labour or Tory?'

'Lib Dem! He's a Cornishman, isn't he?'

'Passionate about it?'

'Mm. A bit. He can be quite fiery – but then Jodie could be, too. I think they used to have the odd fight, but they were never serious and always over very quickly. Neither of them bore grudges.'

'And were you all at school together?'

'Lord, no – Tom's a good four years older than Jodie or me, but we all lived in Trenellack so we knew each other all our lives. Jodie always liked him – well, hero-worshipped, really – and he always had a soft spot for her.' I shot him a glance. 'Why all the questions?'

'Just wanted to know the background.'

'You're not still thinking that Tom . . .?'

'I'm not thinking anything! I just want to know how it was you were all so close.'

'If you hadn't been away at boarding school you could have been in our gang too.'

'Yes.' He grinned at me. 'And who knows? *You* might have hero-worshipped *me*.'

'Sorry. In those days I had no room in my life for anyone but Jason Donovan.' I laughed at the thought. 'How sad is that?'

'I was an Olivia Newton-John man myself. I modelled myself on John Travolta just in case the opportunity arose to drag her on to the dance floor. I rather fancied myself as a mover and groover.'

'Now that I would like to see.'

We were laughing, but sobered rapidly as he pulled up outside Tom's house. Nothing seemed funny any more. We exchanged nervous glances, took deep breaths and opened the car doors, the moment lightened only by Jamie's delight at being released from his chair.

Tom must have seen us coming, as he opened the front door before we reached it. Before saying a word I put my arms around him and for a moment we clung together. He looked gaunt and strained and much older than his thirty years, but he held out a friendly hand to Ian and ushered us all into the house.

I was glad Ian was there, and Jamie too, for I was finding it overwhelmingly sad to be among all Jodie's things: the curtains I'd helped her choose in Plymouth, the books we'd both enjoyed, the wedding photograph on the mantelpiece. It took me a moment or two to pull myself together, and meanwhile Ian took charge of the situation, handing over the few things I had found in the desk drawer and managing to do so with the maximum amount of tact and sensitivity.

'There was also something else I found,' I said at last, a little awkwardly. My manner must have alerted Tom to expect something unusual, for he looked up at me sharply.

'Oh?'

'She left this disk with all your household stuff on it. And a letter, Tom. I couldn't help seeing it and I took the liberty of printing it out. It seemed important.'

'What letter?'

'Addressed to me, though I never received it,' Ian said. 'Jodie seemed to think she needed to consult a solicitor – here, take a look for yourself.'

He had the copy of the letter I'd sent him and this he handed over to Tom, who read it in silence with his frown growing deeper.

'She mentioned nothing of this to me,' he said when he had finished. 'I can't imagine what she had in mind. You say she never sent it?'

'I certainly never received it.'

'Maybe – well, maybe she found it wasn't necessary after all, and just forgot to delete it.' Tom continued to look bewildered, however. 'It must be something to do with the hotel, surely? Something illegal she suspected? The Ransleighs cooking the books, or something?'

Jamie was getting restless at all this serious adult chat

and began agitating for some diversion. I hushed him and produced a few small toys from my bag which quietened him, though not for long, I guessed.

'I suppose it could be,' Ian said. 'But what Prue and I don't understand is why she didn't just report it to the police. Why write to me?'

'And why it was so crucial that she saw Ian by Wednesday?' I added. 'Bearing in mind that—' I paused, not wanting to mention Jodie's death.

'She died on Thursday.' In a flat voice Tom completed my sentence. 'You think this is connected, then?'

'I thought it just might be.'

'I don't see how—' He paused, trying to make sense of what I had said. 'You mean someone might have – might have contrived the accident? *Murdered* her?'

'Well, it did occur to us. It seemed so coincidental that she should be frantically worried about something illegal one moment and – not able to do anything about it the next.'

Tom read the letter once more.

'The police will have to see this,' he said. 'But I can't believe it was anything but an accident. The cliff path was unstable. It was roped off and there were notices. The inquest didn't leave any room for doubt; it was an accident of her own making.'

'I just can't see her taking that risk when she knew the danger,' I said.

Tom gave a brief, mirthless breath of laughter.

'No?'

'But, *why*?' I asked helplessly.

'Because she was Jodie, that's why, doing what Jodie always did. You know what she was like, Prue – she was always impulsive, never liked to be warned not to do something. I truly believe the verdict of the inquest. It was an accident, pure and simple.'

'But we've all been brought up not to take risks with a cliff fall—'

'I know, I know. But she wanted to take the short way home and nothing was going to stop her. She could be so stubborn sometimes.'

'Yes, I suppose she could,' I said doubtfully.

'You must know she could! And if you didn't – well, maybe you didn't know her as well as you imagined.'

This had been what Sean had implied, and was not a welcome thought to me.

'She was stubborn in good ways,' I said. 'She wouldn't let herself be beaten by anything.'

'That's what I mean,' Tom said. 'She wouldn't be put off by warning notices if it was something she wanted to do. You haven't seen her white-water rafting – or skiing, come to that. I can tell you, Prue, there were times when she scared the hell out of me, especially when she was in a bit of a mood. Which she could be – you know that, too.'

I didn't argue with him. He was right. I had felt nothing but affection for Jodie and knew I would miss her for always. She was a beautiful, funny, vivacious girl and a good friend, but she had her faults the same as the rest of us, and a tendency to moodiness was one of them.

'And was she in a bit of a mood that Thursday?' I asked, very softly.

Tom was biting his lip, as if his memories were far from pleasant.

'Yes, she was,' he said at last. 'She was put out because she said I hadn't warned her I needed to borrow her car. I'd put mine in the garage for a couple of days, having the wing straightened after some fool driver crashed into me, but I had to go to Penzance that day for an absolutely essential meeting that had cropped up at the last minute. I said I'd drop her off in the morning, but that it wouldn't hurt her to walk home for once.' He closed his eyes for a second, as if reliving every sharp word that had passed between them. 'I swear I'd mentioned it days before, but she said I hadn't. She said—' He took a breath. 'She said didn't I realise the cliff path was closed and she'd have to walk the long way round.' His face was turned away from us, his mouth working furiously. 'And I said – I said—' He struggled to keep his voice under control. 'I said that was too bad, but I didn't really care if she had to swim home. I still needed the car, unless she wanted me to lose a very big commission.'

'Oh, Tom,' I said. 'Don't beat yourself up about it. Everyone says things they don't mean. Jodie as much as anyone.'

He turned and looked at me, and I don't think I've ever seen such misery on anyone's face.

'So that, more or less, is the mood in which we parted. I sort of calmed down and apologised before she got out of the car to go into work, but I think she could easily have thought, To hell with him, he doesn't give a damn for me or tell me anything. What does it matter if I walk along the cliff path, dangerous or not?'

'She had no reason to think that,' I said.

'I can't agree with you. I wish I could.' His voice was husky and barely audible. 'I admit to being very abstracted in the days before – before she died. There was a lot of stress at work: a contract lost through sheer incompetence – not mine, exactly, but something I had to carry the can for. You know how it is . . .' He sat, biting his lip for a moment, and the only sound in the room was Jamie, making *brrm-brrm* car noises and playing with his toys. 'I know I shouldn't have brought my troubles home with me, or having done so I should have talked things over with her,' he went on. 'Explained myself. Told her what was going on in my life. But I didn't. I just shut her out. We didn't talk much at all that last week. Neither of us was behaving in a rational, normal kind of way. She must have been worried about all this stuff she wrote about in the letter, but I was so uptight I didn't notice it.'

It was torturing him, talking like this. I got up and went over to him, putting my hands on his shoulders.

'Stop it, Tom. Stop it. Jodie loved you. You know she did. You had a happy marriage. I would have known if there was anything seriously wrong.'

But would I? Would I?

'Yeah.' His expression was bleak, his voice dismissive.

'And you loved her. She was never in any doubt of that.'

'I hope you're right.' He passed a hand over his face as if making an effort to achieve normality. 'I feel I failed her. I know I failed her.'

'That's nonsense. Everyone has good and bad times. You know perfectly well that given a few days all this would have blown over and you'd have been making all sorts of plans for the future.'

'Maybe. I could sometimes give a pretty convincing impression of a complete bastard, though.'

'Nobody thinks that of you.'

'No?' He gave me a wry look. 'Well, I hope you're right. Thanks anyway, Prue. You're a good friend. You'll be at the funeral on Tuesday?'

'Yes, of course.'

'There's a service in the church at two.'

'I'll be there.'

He folded the letter and put it in his pocket.

'I'll see the police get this,' he said.

We left shortly after that and drove in silence for a while.

'You're right, he is a nice guy,' Ian said at last. 'I think feelings of guilt are pretty run-of-the-mill when someone dies. There's always the feeling that something more should have been said or done.'

'He's right about Jodie,' I said. 'She was stubborn. But like I said to Tom, it was usually in a good way. The sort of way that made her never give up whatever she set herself to do.'

'And moody?'

'Well, sometimes. She could be. No more than most.'

Was now the time to tell him what Sean had said about her? I didn't want to. Enough bad things had been said about Jodie already that morning and I didn't want him to get the wrong impression. In any case, it wasn't true. I was pretty sure of that.

So I said nothing – and by now we were arriving at the Ship Inn. Jamie was unusually quiet, a little overawed at being taken into the restaurant, until he was seated in his high chair with a likeness of Tigger on the tray provided by the obliging management. He was entranced by all the ship's paraphernalia that was in the room – the green and red ship's lanterns, the draped fishing nets, the brass ship's wheel that was mounted on the wall. I would like to say they kept him quiet, but it proved to be quite the opposite; he insisted on exclaiming with delight at all of it, twisting in his chair and vociferously drawing our attention to things that caught his eye.

'Mummy – Eem – lights!' Eem was the nearest Jamie could get to 'Ian' – to whom, I thought, great credit was due for coping with this demanding presence so equably. He appeared to have accepted quite cheerfully the fact that sustained adult conversation is all but impossible when one is accompanied by a lively twenty-two-month-old child.

Food arrived, and Jamie gave up his running commentary in order to devote his attention to it, demanding, at length, that only Eem should have the privilege of wiping his gravy-stained face. Ian solemnly complied, just as a sweet old lady passed the table on her way out and paused to beam at us.

'What a dear little chap,' she said. 'A great credit to you both, if I may say so.'

I thanked her. She clearly thought that we were a family, but neither of us appeared to think it worth correcting her, though we exchanged amused and slightly self-conscious smiles as she went on her way.

We left the restaurant ourselves shortly afterwards, and drove back to the farm to return the car to Mary. Then, because it was such a fine day, I changed Jamie's best shoes for his wellies, picked up his plastic bucket and spade, and the three of us walked down the valley path to the beach. Jamie was between us, holding a hand of each, demanding to be swung back and forth, which we did with enthusiasm for a while. The exercise palled, however, and knowing he could come to no harm I let him run wild.

Below us, to the left, the hotel looked as if it were dreaming peacefully in the spring sunshine. With one accord we stopped and looked at it for a moment. The grey stone, the blueish slate roof, the shape of the house and outbuildings, seemed so in harmony with their surroundings that one could almost imagine it had grown there naturally. The gardens surrounding it were at their best at this time of the year, a riot of rhododendrons and azaleas, pinks and whites and reds.

'I always vowed I'd own that place when I grew up,' I said. 'I was going to scour the world for a millionaire and kindly allow him to marry me, on the condition that he came to live at Boscothey Manor.' I laughed at the notion. 'Oh well, maybe working there is the next best thing.' But still I looked at it. 'It must have seen so much history – tragic and peaceful, sad and happy—'

'The lot, no doubt,' Ian said. 'Forgive the cliché, but it's a pity the walls can't speak. Maybe they could answer a few of our present-day questions.'

'Maybe.'

Jamie came running up with a fistful of grasses, which he thrust at me before tearing off again in the general direction of the beach. 'Why Friday?' I said as we followed him. 'Why was Friday going to be too late? Who, under that roof down there, knows what the hell Jodie was worried about?'

'What about guests?' Ian said. 'Could someone have been due to arrive then – someone who posed some sort of a threat?'

'I wonder?' I thought about it and shrugged my shoulders. 'I suppose anything's possible.'

'But Wednesday was the deadline, wasn't it? She had to see me before Wednesday, because that was when she was expecting something to happen. Is there an office diary you could look up?'

'Yes, of course, but it's only for Paul and Delia's business appointments, or the arrival of VIPs. Nothing personal. It's my job to keep it up to date.'

'And presumably Jodie did the same.'

'She did. I've already looked back and can't see anything that seems at all out of the ordinary. I'll have another look, though, just in case I missed anything.'

We'd arrived at the beach by this time and all talk of Jodie was shelved as Ian threw himself into amusing Jamie. He made sandcastles that were enthusiastically jumped on and invented a simplified hopscotch that both of them seemed to enjoy. But on the whole Jamie needed no entertainment and was content to run down to the water's edge, where he filled his little bucket with stones, then hauled it back with great care to where Ian and I had retired to a flat slab of rock, sheltered from the wind.

He then emptied the bucket at our feet, where the pile of stones grew larger and larger.

We applauded his efforts with great enthusiasm and kept asking for more since, as long as this game lasted, it demanded little effort on our part. It was very pleasant there, out of the wind, with a spasmodic sun warm on our faces.

'He's a great little guy,' Ian said, watching Jamie's sturdy legs encased in their rolled-up denims and red wellies twinkling down the beach. He gave a brief, self-conscious laugh. 'You know, Prue, I felt ridiculously, unjustifiably proud when that woman spoke to us in the pub, just as if I had a right to any of the credit. You're doing a terrific job with him.'

'Thanks.' There was a sudden awkward silence, during which words seemed to be hovering on the brink of being spoken. His right hand was on the rock beside mine, only centimetres away, and suddenly I was very conscious of the shape and the strength of it.

Far down the beach, another child was playing with his parents and his cries were borne faintly to us on the breeze. Gulls shrieked overhead and the sound of the waves as they surged and retreated made a soothing back-drop to a strangely charged moment.

It seemed a lifetime since I had felt any man's touch – until, of course, Sean's attempts to hold me the other night. I'd felt nothing but revulsion on that occasion. I'd made it so clear that I wasn't up for it, but he'd taken no notice; what else, as he had said himself, was there to do in this God-forsaken part of the country? I suppose I'd seemed fair game, just as Mandy was.

But now, suddenly, it was as if Sean had set in motion some process that had been broken and inoperable for the past two years. I wanted Ian – wanted him to touch me, to hold me. Wanted it so much and so suddenly that

I felt I must be vibrating with longing. I wasn't thinking of where it might lead, or how I felt about him. I simply wanted him, and there must have been some evidence of it in my eyes when I turned to look at him, for I saw him blink as if he were confused at what he could see. And no wonder, for my relationship with him had only ever been one of friendship. Occasionally he had made the odd flirtatious remark, which I had always lightly rebuffed. It had been a joke, no more. Now I was sending out a message that said it was a joke no longer.

'I don't suppose you've heard anything from Jamie's dad?' Ian said.

It took me a second to adjust my mind to take in the question. Why was he talking about Kit now?

'No.'

'I've instituted a few enquiries, without any result. It would be a good thing if you could get the divorce tied up.'

'I suppose so,' I said. I must have sounded lukewarm, for he looked at me with a puzzled expression, as if he wasn't sure he was reading the message aright. 'You do want a divorce, don't you?'

Jamie came and dumped another bucketful of pebbles before I could answer, chattered for a moment or two and was off again. Ian's eyes were on him when he spoke again.

'If Kit came back . . . if he said he wanted a fresh start – would you agree?'

'No! Absolutely not!'

'Stranger things have happened.'

'And you've seen it all, of course.' My words were edged with sarcasm. I could hear the hardness of them, which must have contrasted sharply with the way I'd looked at him only moments before. Thinking about Kit always had the effect of turning my emotions to ice. That strangely peaceful, pregnant moment had totally disintegrated, as if it had never happened.

'You're right.' Ian picked up a pebble and skittered it away. 'I have seen it all – and on the whole I admit it's given me a very jaundiced view of marriage. I'm constantly amazed by the way love can turn to hate the way it does. Presumably all the warring couples I see in the course of my duties loved each other once, or why the hell did they get together in the first place? Presumably their hearts beat faster and they swooned with joy in each other's arms, yet a few years down the line they hate each other's guts.'

I didn't speak for some moments.

'They call it sex,' I said eventually. 'You can be blind to a man's faults if you want him enough.'

'True,' he admitted. 'And a pretty face can mask a multitude of sins.'

'That sounded like the voice of experience.'

He laughed at that. 'Several experiences, in fact.'

'Then you know what I'm talking about. The scales can fall from your eyes and you realise that the person you thought you loved is a total stranger. Believe me, I've been there and it's shattering. As for getting back with Kit again, I can't imagine why you think there's the slightest chance of it. I couldn't ever trust him again. In fact—' I paused, and when I spoke it was as if I were speaking to myself. 'Trusting anyone again, in that way, seems almost impossible.'

'We're both pretty hopeless cases, aren't we?' Ian said. 'Yet it works for some people. Mary and Roger, for example, and my own parents—'

'And Jodie and Tom,' I said. 'I swear they were rock-solid really, in spite of odd fights and misunderstandings.'

Ian was quiet for a few moments, and I imagined he was thinking of Tom, wondering if his and Jodie's marriage was as unshakeable as I had thought. Was this the moment to tell him about Sean and Jodie? No – not now, or ever. It wasn't true and I was going to dismiss it from my mind.

When at last he spoke, his words had nothing to do with Tom. He turned me towards him.

'Prue,' he said. 'Is there the slightest chance it would work for us? I keep thinking it could, even though I come over like a poor bastard who's terrified of commitment. You must know how much I think of you. How I've wanted to—'

I didn't let him finish but jumped to my feet, not even trying to make sense of the fact that only moments ago I wanted to feel him close to me. I wasn't ready for this, even though for one crazy second it had seemed a possibility. Knowing him as I did, I was certain that any relationship would be serious and lasting, maybe because of all the misery he had witnessed. The thought of that kind of commitment frightened me to death.

'No. No. I'm sorry—' I brushed sand from my skirt. 'We must go. It's getting cold and anyway, I can't deal with this sort of stuff. Don't get heavy, Ian, please. Just be a friend, that's all I want.'

It was true that the warmth of the sun had lessened now, but it was a different kind of cold that had me in its grip. I was cold with a panic that swamped me like the incoming tide.

I didn't wait to see the effect of my words, but hurried down the beach, calling to Jamie. I seemed to know instinctively that Ian would still be sitting on the rock looking after me. What expression was he wearing, I wondered. Relief? Exasperation? Disappointment? Amusement? Maybe he was back there laughing at me because I'd totally misunderstood him.

But I hadn't. I knew I hadn't. It might not have developed into a proposal in the old, down-on-one-knee, accepted sense of the word, but he had definitely been shaping up to a proposition of some sort – and one thing I was certain of: we were both hopelessly wary and unsure of ourselves, he almost as much as I.

Poor us, I thought as I collected Jamie and coerced him back to where Ian still waited for us. Poor us.

Six

When I arrived at the hotel the following morning, I found Paul and Delia in a state bordering on panic. A big wedding was taking place on the Saturday of that week – the 'It' girl Kiki Jephson to the fabulously wealthy media tycoon Gerry Gainsford – with guests arriving from London and New York and various other points on the globe, filling every available room in the hotel, and all bed-and-breakfast accommodation for miles around taken by the attendant paparazzi.

The only room in the hotel not pressed into service was the Sunflower Room, which was out of use due to a massive refurbishment programme. Not only had it been divested of its beds and all soft furnishings, but the bathroom was no more than an empty shell, needing retiling and a completely new bathroom suite. Now Lady Jephson, the highly autocratic mother of the bride who had been on the phone constantly checking every detail of food and decor, had contacted reception to say that another four guests had, somehow, to be accommodated.

The Ransleighs were busy poring over the room plan in Paul's inner sanctum, having by the sound of it their own separate nervous breakdowns, when Isobel put her head round my door and, shaken out of her usual reserve, was sufficiently fired up by the drama to bring me up to date with the cause of it.

'I can't imagine how they're going to sort it out,' she

said, her voice lowered. 'Sunflower's going to take an army of decorators to get it ready in time, and the last I heard, the bathroom suite is still on the high seas. Naturally it's not one of your average bathrooms. They can't just pop down to B&Q for a replacement!'

'So what's going to happen?'

'Well, I told Lady Jephson we were completely full, but she refused to take it in. I thought she was going to have a fit! She even threatened to cancel the whole thing – said we simply had to *make* room.' She rolled her eyes as if in despair. 'Did she imagine we could run up an extension before Saturday, or conjure bathroom suites out of the air? Luckily Paul was standing right beside me when the call came through, so as soon as she got stroppy I handed the whole thing over to him. He is the boss, after all. Let him take care of it.'

'They should call her bluff,' I said. 'She'd never get anywhere else to put on such a big affair at this late stage. Good heavens – there are only five days left!'

'I don't know about that. Think of the publicity! There's a rumour that *Hello!*'s paying for the lot, so really you could say it was a make-or-break deal. The Jephsons bring a lot of business here as it is, so Delia will jump through hoops to avoid offending them. Still, if we're full, then we're full. You'd think she could understand that.'

With that she departed, leaving me to reflect that every cloud had a silver lining. Paul and Delia might look on this as a disaster, but at least Isobel was speaking to me at last.

I could certainly appreciate the problem, and I was glad it didn't fall to me to sort it out. It wasn't as if there were a comparable hotel anywhere close by that could be used to take the overflow. Boscothey Manor was one of a kind, certainly in this area, and every other acceptable bed-space in this part of the county was already booked.

Flicking a glance towards the inner office, where the Ransleigh altercation was clearly audible, I decided to ignore that day's troubles for as long as possible. It would be a good opportunity to leaf through the diary once more, just to check that I had missed nothing momentous on the previous occasion. I turned the pages back to that dramatic week at the beginning of March, but still could find nothing to indicate that anything unusual had taken place. On Thursday, 2 March, the day that Jodie had written the letter, the only events apparently worth recording were a dental appointment at 3.30, made on Delia's behalf, and a delivery of oil – *p.m.*, it said, no particular time specified. All the hotel's heating was run on oil as there was no mains gas piped anywhere nearer than St Venn.

The weekend that followed also seemed to be devoid of any VIP guests and there was nothing entered until Monday, when it appeared that Paul was seeing a market gardener who had applied to supply the hotel with vegetables. Later in the day was noted the expected arrival of a Lord and Lady Altwich – obvious candidates for the red-carpet treatment.

On the Wednesday which had seemed so important in Jodie's eyes, Paul had a meeting with the tourist board in Truro at 10.30, followed by a lunchtime meeting at the Eden Project, which I happened to know was concerning special out-of-hours visits by guests of the hotel. And by that time Jodie would already have met with her fatal accident.

On the following day, Thursday, there was a scribble in Paul's writing indicating that he was going to London. Could that be significant, I wondered? Was Jodie anxious to make contact with Ian before Paul left? It was a possibility, but on the other hand Paul had mentioned to me at my interview that he was required to go to town from

time to time for meetings with the owners of this particular hotel group, so there seemed nothing remarkable
about this entry either.

On the face of it, all appeared totally innocent – but, I
said to myself, it would, wouldn't it? If there were any
secrets to be discovered, they would hardly be here. They
would be safe in Paul's apartment, or perhaps locked in
the desk in his inner office. Though most of the hotel
keys were kept in the cabinet in my office, those to his
desk were kept on a big bunch together with his car keys,
apartment keys and various others.

Jokes abounded at the hotel about the way he locked
that desk so carefully. Carol said it was her guess he kept
a pile of dirty magazines in the bottom drawer, but Sean
said it was more likely to be a little black book full of
names and addresses he required when in London. (And
who wouldn't need it, married to Delia? he demanded.)

I had never investigated whether he guarded it as jeal-
ously as people said. I knew that he often locked it when
he was going out – I had seen him doing it – but I didn't
know if this happened every time or if he sometimes
forgot, or just didn't bother. It had never interested me
before – but it did now, and I resolved, if ever I knew
him to be out of the way, to do a bit of snooping. I didn't
welcome the thought one bit: quite apart from finding it
a tacky thing to do, I was very aware that if caught in
the act I would be likely to lose not only Paul's trust but
this very congenial job. Half of me hoped the opportunity would never arise.

But now, as things stood, I had nothing new to tell Ian
except that Paul had scheduled a trip to London on the
Thursday of Jodie's death. And after the way I'd treated
him, I doubted if he would be interested in hearing from
me anyway.

Our parting the previous day had been a little awkward

and undoubtedly on the cool side, and thinking about it afterwards I felt guilty and regretful. The day had been a good one until I panicked so wildly at the end of it – cutting him off in mid-sentence, acting like a fourteen-year-old. I hadn't been fair to him. I should at least have heard him out, I thought now. After putting himself out to listen to my worries concerning Jodie, after playing with my son, taking us to lunch and being a general support to me over the last few months, it seemed the least I could have done was to treat him with respect, not leap to my feet and stride away as if he had offended me. I had no explanation for my impulse to flee, except that I wasn't ready yet – not for Ian, not for any man. But I hated to think that I'd hurt him.

Voices from the inner office brought me back to the here and now. Delia was getting progressively louder. She was clearly in the worst of tempers, while Paul was doing his best to calm her down.

'The old bag won't cancel,' I heard him say soothingly, clearly referring to the demanding Lady Jephson. 'She's in too deep now. I'll get on to the plumbers and the decorators—'

'That's still only half the answer. Four more people, she said. Even if we get Sunflower up and running, we need another room.'

'There are some kids coming, aren't there? They can surely bunk up together in Camellia. It's quite big enough to take a couple more beds.'

'Paul, will you *please* pay attention? We can't do that! There are boys and girls coming, all teenagers – there's no way they can go in together.'

'Then the two singles will have to double up.'

'For God's sake use your head! Two of them are *millionaires*! From *America*! They're both connected to tourism in some way, so Lady Jephson said. We have to impress them, and we won't do that by sticking them in a boys' dormitory.'

'I don't know about that. Might remind them of their schooldays.'

'*Will* you stop being such a fool!'

I kept my head down and got on with some letters I had left over from Friday. After a bit, Delia, still haranguing Paul as if the whole thing had been his fault from beginning to end, swept through my office and out to the front hall, high heels clicking as if to underline her agitation. Paul, following closely behind, pulled a face at me *en passant*.

'I may be gone some time,' he said in a theatrically sepulchral kind of voice.

I suppressed a giggle and kept on with what I was doing until suddenly a thought struck me. This might – just *might* – be the one day that Paul had forgotten to lock his desk when he left the room. He'd certainly been distracted enough, but I felt uncertain about investigating the point as I had no idea how long he would be away from the office.

But it did seem to be a now-or-never situation. Slowly, not really wanting to, I got up from my desk and, with a quick glance over my shoulder to see that the coast was clear, went into his office. The desk was slanted across the far corner of the room, taking up the greater part of it. It was heavy and impressive, a Regency reproduction, with one long drawer across the top and a section on either side with three drawers in each, one key at the top serving to unlock them all. With a catch of my breath I saw that I'd guessed right. He hadn't bothered to lock it. The whole bunch of keys was dangling there, the appropriate one still in the keyhole of the long top drawer.

He said he might be some time. He'd meant it as a joke, judging by the manner of its delivery, and it probably meant nothing; he could be back at any second. But when would I ever have another opportunity like this? My heart was in my mouth as, with another glance towards the door, I opened the drawer. There wasn't much inside: a silver paper-knife, a chequebook, a few biros and paperclips, a book of tide tables which he needed when guests wanted to use the hotel boat. Nothing else.

I closed it and tried the top small drawer: nothing but hotel notepaper and envelopes. I shut it swiftly and went on to the next one, thinking it would help a great deal if I knew exactly what I was looking for.

Perhaps this, I thought, as I looked down at the contents of the third drawer, for there, the present month of March uppermost, was a calendar of the kind that can be bought from any stationer for very little, a month to a page, each day allotted a square.

Only on one day was there an entry of any kind. In the square allotted to 8 March was written a time: 2.30. I thought back to the main diary in my office. That, surely, was the day Paul was going to the Eden Project for a lunchtime meeting. What was happening at 2.30? Would he be back at the hotel by then? It didn't seem likely. It would take at least twenty minutes to drive from Eden, probably more, and they were bound to sit over lunch.

Could it mean anything else? I couldn't imagine so, but I stood and puzzled over it for a second. I took the calendar out of the drawer and turned back to the previous month. And there, on 11 February, was a similar pencilled entry, only this time it was 1.35.

I heard the door of my outer office open and quickly I replaced the calendar and closed the drawer. In my haste, I allowed it to make a slight click and I looked fearfully towards the door with my heart beating several times faster than usual, as if I were about to be discovered in an act of grand larceny.

Thank heaven it was only Sean who appeared in the doorway. How I would have explained my interest in the desk to Paul, I couldn't think.

Even so, he seemed to suspect something.

'And what,' he said, 'might you be up to? Looking for the dirty magazines?'

I took a breath and directed an impersonal smile in his direction, moving towards him with what I hoped looked like casual confidence. Ever since the evening he'd taken me out to dinner, we had been distant with each other, managing to avoid any one-to-one contact. I had seen him in the kitchen, of course, but had made sure that I was always deep in conversation with one of the others. It was unusual to see him in this part of the hotel.

'Hello, Sean,' I said coolly. 'I'm just going about my secretarial duties.'

'Really? I thought you looked the picture of guilt.'

I laughed with what I hoped sounded like innocent amusement.

'What nonsense! You startled me, that's all. What are you doing here?'

'I was sent for.' He stood aside as I passed him to go into my office. 'Some people actively desire my company, believe it or not.'

'Sean—' I paused, wanting to clear the air. 'Let's just draw a line under the other evening, OK?'

He leaned casually against the door-jamb, arms folded, handsome as ever even in his cook's whites.

'Well, I bear no ill-will,' he said.

I stared at him in disbelief and gave an incredulous breath of laughter.

'How awfully good of you.'

'I'm like that. The forgiving sort.'

The nerve of it! What had he to forgive? I opened my mouth to protest at this, but then I closed it again and turned away from him, picking up a pile of papers and going over to the filing cabinet.

'I don't know how long Paul will be,' I said. 'Maybe you should come back later.'

'I'll wait,' he said. 'Sure, the view from here is a very pleasant one.'

I made the mistake of looking round. His eyes were on me, mocking me.

'Why do you do it, Sean?' I asked him, half amused in spite of everything. 'It's really very corny and it doesn't cut any ice with me.'

He lifted his hands as if in surrender, his blue eyes wide with surprise.

'Sure now, what have I said to deserve that?'

I could think of a number of things, not least the fact that he had deliberately tried to blacken Jodie's memory, but I'd said we would draw a line under that and I intended to keep to it.

'Forget it,' I said. 'But please, if you're going to wait for Paul here, could you just sit down and keep quiet? I have work to do.'

I returned to my filing, but it wasn't in him to keep his mouth shut for long.

'This – antipathy of yours,' he said. 'I can't see the reason for it. You'd think I'd raped you—'

I slammed the filing cabinet drawer shut, my anger boiling over.

'You weren't too ready to take no for an answer, were you? But that's not why I'm angry with you, and you know it.'

'I don't think I do.'

'Then you should. You seem to think that just because Jodie's dead it doesn't matter what lies you tell about her.'

'We were close. That's all I said.'

'You implied more. And listen to me, Sean. If any word of what you said gets to Tom, I personally will—'

I came to a halt. He was laughing at me now, for he knew and I knew that there was nothing I could do to exact any revenge.

'Seriously,' he said. 'You are over-reacting – reading far more into it than I meant. Jodie and I – well, we were good friends. Very good friends. I had no intention of implying anything else.'

'OK, let's leave it at that,' I said after a moment, knowing that he was still lying. There was no point in arguing about it. I had heard what he said and the tone of voice he said it in, and I knew that it was meant to upset and unsettle me; revenge, I supposed, for telling him I wasn't interested in his amorous advances.

It was at this moment that Paul came back, looking pleased with himself.

'Panic over,' he said. 'I've threatened the plumbers with death and destruction if they don't get over here this very afternoon to finish the plumbing in the Sunflower Room. *And* do the tiling *and* fit the new bath and basin. It won't be the all-singing, all-dancing affair that Delia ordered, but she's going over there right now to choose a bathroom suite from stock and I expect it'll be perfectly acceptable. Then tomorrow the decorators have promised to be here at the crack of dawn. The furnishings are Delia's department, so I'm leaving the worrying to her.'

'I thought you needed two extra rooms,' Sean said.

'Ah – glad you mentioned it, Sean. I was about to break the news. You'll have to move in with Gaston for a couple of nights. Move your things tonight, will you? That will mean the decorators can get busy on your room tomorrow or the next day, to make it fit for a couple of the kids. You'll agree it was due for a lick of paint.'

'But – but . . .' In his outrage, Sean could hardly speak. Paul patted his shoulder in a fatherly manner. 'You can choose the colour,' he said. 'Within reason. Now come through and we'll have our chat.'

The inner door was closed behind them, leaving me feeling unworthily amused at Sean's impotent fury. I got on with my work, but couldn't help speculating about the reason for Sean's visit. Was he getting promotion? More pay? Or had he blotted his copybook in some way? It wasn't out of the question, knowing Sean.

The following day brought with it the sadness of Jodie's funeral. I was half expecting Ian to ring me and suggest that we go together; and if he did, I told myself, I would make amends. Ask him to supper. Tell him I really wanted to be friends, it was just that I wasn't ready for any kind of intimate relationship.

I heard no word from him, however, and because Mary was working and unable to get away, I went on my own. It didn't matter. The church was almost full, as everyone had known and liked Jodie, and I was well acquainted with almost everyone present.

I took my seat halfway down the left-hand side with some other old friends. As the organ played softly I looked at the lovely window above the altar and the ruby and sapphire light filtering through it; the grey stone pillars carved with acanthus leaves; the vaulted roof. There was something calming and comforting in the very familiarity of these surroundings. Both Jodie and I had been married here, as well as many of our friends, and here my mother's funeral service had taken place. Sad occasions and joyful occasions – all had been experienced here. It was part of life and part of death and as I sat there I was acutely conscious of the transience of it all. Don't waste it, an inner voice seemed to say.

It was only when I came out of the church that I saw

that Ian had been there all the time. He must have slipped in at the back just before the service started.

He came over and greeted me – in a reserved sort of way, I thought, but perhaps that was only because of the solemnity and sadness of the occasion. We exchanged a few stilted words about the music and the large number who had come to the church before he looked at his watch.

'Forgive me,' he said. 'I've got to dash. There's a meeting—'

'Wait, Ian.' I caught at his arm. 'About Sunday. I'm so sorry—'

'You've nothing to be sorry for. I was the one who spoke out of turn.'

'It was such a lovely day.'

'Yes – yes, it was. But I must fly. I'll be in touch about the letter. Let you know what's going on.'

Already he was walking away from me, down to the lych-gate to where I could see his car parked outside. I stood and watched him go, aware that something had gone out of our relationship. There didn't appear to be a lot I could do about it; not at the moment, anyway.

It was a sad day altogether. Paul had come to the church, representing the hotel, but Delia had stayed away. And so had Sean, for all the talk of his friendship with Jodie. He simply couldn't bear it, I heard him saying to the kitchen at large the day before. He hated funerals.

It occurred to me to wonder if he thought the rest of the population enjoyed them. Personally, I found the whole occasion the most depressing thing I had ever known. Tom looked haunted, as if he were still racked by the feeling of guilt that he couldn't rationalise away.

Such a tragedy, everyone said. Such a dreadful waste of a young life.

But, as it always does, life went on. The Jephson wedding passed off without mishap. Not that I saw any of it. It was the talk of the village, I gathered, and quite a number of local people went to stand outside the church, hoping to catch a glimpse of the bride, but I had more than enough to do at home and, truth to tell, had had my fill of the wretched wedding long before the weekend.

Isobel gave me a blow-by-blow account of the whole thing on Monday morning. The bride looked beautiful, she reported, and her mother, though resembling nothing more than a ship in full sail, seemed satisfied with the last-minute arrangements. The Sunflower Room had been finished in the nick of time; the two boys who were sleeping in Sean's room had been quite happy with their unexpected quarters; and Sean, she told me, though officially sharing with Gaston, had actually moved in with the accommodating Mandy for the two nights in question.

Easter was early that year and was now upon us, marking the true beginning of the tourist season. There was almost a tangible feeling of urgency and tension in the hotel, of the kind that one can feel before the start of a play. The curtain was about to go up on the busiest time of the year. More seasonal staff had been engaged. The furnishings and fittings in every room, already immaculate, had to be inspected all over again. Every piece of equipment was checked to ensure that all was in working order.

Gaston became ever more Gallic and unpredictable, and Delia's nerves were almost at breaking point. If she wasn't haranguing the cleaners she was bickering with Paul. I did my best to keep out of her way as much as possible. The car park began to fill up with glitzy cars – Mercedes, BMWs, the odd Porsche and a Rolls-Royce. And though our clientele was not of the kind to make the place echo with shouts of revelry, there was a pleasing buzz, as if the old manor was coming to life. This, I thought, was how it was meant to be, this mixture of well-bred voices in conversation, laughter, and the clink of glasses and cutlery.

Jodie's letter was still on my mind and I was puzzled by the fact that though Ian had said he would keep me informed, I had heard nothing from him, and nothing from Tom either. A couple of weeks after Easter, and after much hesitation on my part, I phoned him to tell him of the second calendar I had discovered, with its unexplained figures beside 8 March, the date that Jodie had considered so important. I also told him that Paul had apparently gone to London the day after.

'And there was also a time written in for 11 February,' I told him. 'One thirty-five.'

'A.m. or p.m.?' He sounded strangely remote and impersonal.

'It didn't say.'

'Anything for April?'

'I didn't have time to look.'

There was a short, and I hoped thoughtful, silence.

'It could be a personal appointment of some kind,' he said. 'Golf, maybe? Or a lady?'

'Anything's possible,' I said. I felt dispirited. It seemed clear to me, just from the sound of his voice, that he didn't think these numbers had any meaning worth pursuing. 'Have you heard anything from Tom about the letter?' I asked. 'Do you know if he's shown it to the police?'

'Yes, he has,' Ian said. 'It's apparently all in hand. Nothing left for me to do. Or you,' he added, in the kind of manner that made me feel I was sticking my nose in where it wasn't wanted. 'So – ' his voice took on a heartier tone – 'are you well, Prue?'

'Fine, thanks.'

'And Jamie?'

'Fine.' I had the strong impression that he was trying

to change the subject. 'Listen,' I said. 'You will keep me informed if you find out anything, won't you, Ian?'

'Yes, of course I will. And don't worry, Prue. Just take care of yourself.'

You can tell a lot from a disembodied voice on the phone, and it seemed to me that these were the first words he had spoken that had any genuine warmth in them. An invitation to share my supper trembled on my lips, but I said nothing. He might take it the wrong way; he might think I was encouraging him and wanted, after all, something more than friendship. The way my relationship with Sean had deteriorated was surely enough to teach me it wasn't a good idea to make well-meant gestures that could be misinterpreted.

Once more I thought about Jodie and how much I would value a good, long, girls-together chat. She'd always been able to make me laugh, no matter how low my spirits.

They were very low right now.

Seven

After Easter the hotel quietened down a little, but everyone warned me that the lull was only temporary. From about the middle of May things began to get busier again, and from the beginning of June we were fully booked. Some guests, I learned, came annually, reserving the same room from one year to the next, and for all Sean's criticisms, I could see why. The food and service were superb, and nowhere could there be a more beautiful setting. All that was missing was the guarantee of sunshine, but a surprising number of people seemed happy to ignore the possibility of bad weather, of which we had plenty that summer.

If I could be glad about anything concerning Jodie's death, it was the opportunity it gave me to do this job. I didn't kid myself it was important, or socially significant, but I was enjoying it and felt more alive than at any time since I'd embarked on life as a single mother. In some ways, all the staff there seemed like my own family; not that I loved them all, exactly, but we were easy with each other, rejoicing in good times and sympathising in bad. Isobel was inclined to be unpredictable – sometimes friendly, sometimes not – but I had a good working relationship with her. I realised that in spite of her glamorous exterior, she still felt insecure and was suspicious, in the beginning, that I might have some territorial ambitions regarding her job. Nothing could have been further from the truth. My nine-to-five-or-there-abouts hours suited me down to the ground and I would have hated the awkward shiftwork that was the receptionists' lot.

Other members of the staff were turning into real friends, particularly Carol. Even Sean and I had worked out a way of getting on together, being pleasant and polite to each other on the surface. What each thought about the other in private was something else, but we didn't let it show.

I can't say I'd become close to Gaston, but then we were all, including Paul, wary of him. The only person to be totally unaffected by his rages was Benny, the small, balding, far from bright handyman, who put in an appearance in the kitchen from time to time. No matter how vitriolic the swearing, he always grinned and bobbed his white head at Gaston as if he'd received a compliment.

'Dear old chap,' Carol commented, witnessing this one day. 'I don't think he has the nous to realise he's being insulted. He just likes being noticed.'

The rest of us would have liked it better if Gaston had disregarded us altogether. He was too inclined to erupt with Gallic fury for any of us to be comfortable in his presence. Fortunately for most of us it was the kitchen staff who came in for the worst of his rages, but they had learned to treat it all as water off a duck's back.

There seemed no interest on the police's part in what had happened to Jodie – or if there were, I certainly wasn't aware of it. They didn't ask questions; didn't even come to the hotel. I thought that her state of mind in the days preceding her death might have been of concern to them, but it didn't appear so. I could only assume that they had accepted the coroner's verdict unquestioningly. Eventually, not hearing a word from Ian, I rang him to see if he'd had any news, but he merely repeated that as far as he knew it was all in hand.

'But is the case closed?' I persisted.

'I've no idea, Prue. Maybe that's how the police regard it,' he said.

'I've been trying to ring Tom to ask him what's going on, but there's no reply.'

'I gather he's gone to the Bristol office for a while,' Ian said. 'Just for a few months. They wanted him up there for some special job and he thought it might do him good to get away.'

'Perhaps it will. I hope so. You've been in touch with him, then?'

'I happened to run into him in Truro, just before he left.'

'And he hadn't heard if there were any developments?'

'He didn't mention any.'

I thought it was all totally unsatisfactory and I told him so, but he merely uttered some soothing, meaningless remarks that were meant to make me feel that all was for the best in the best of all possible worlds and I wasn't to worry my pretty little head about things that were better left to the experts.

I put the phone down, thinking him the most infuriating man I had ever met; which made little sense in light of the fact that I was missing him. I was damned if I was going to do anything about it, however. I'd made a couple of moves towards him and got nowhere. He knew where to find me if he wanted me.

As for Jodie, though naturally I was absorbed in present-day matters for the most part, my thoughts still turned to that letter from time to time. I couldn't dismiss it as easily as Ian or the police seemed to have done. What was it all about? The question teased me. There had to be a reason for it.

It was during a chat with Isobel over coffee, Jodie's name having been mentioned in quite another context, that I thought to ask her if, in the days before her death, Jodie had seemed worried about anything.

'Jodie? Worried?' Her finely plucked eyebrows rose in astonishment. 'Not that I know of. Little Miss Ray-of-Sunshine, she was – it was enough to drive you crazy sometimes. Nothing seemed to worry her at all – but then we were never that close. I don't believe in getting close to people you work with.'

I'd noticed, I thought, which made it all the more surprising when, one afternoon on the beach with Jamie, she came over and joined us. He took to her at once and they ended up going for a paddle together, much to my amazement. The immaculate Isobel, barefoot with her jeans rolled up, was a sight I had never expected to see.

I was pleased that Carol was, from the beginning, so much more approachable, for being able to chat and share a joke with her lightened the day. I asked her, too, about Jodie's mood in the days leading up to the accident, but she was wasn't able to shed any light on the subject either. She'd had a few days off sick around then, she told me, and had only heard the news about Jodie when she got back to work. I didn't pursue the matter with any of the other members of staff. There didn't seem a lot of point if the police had closed the case.

I was thankful that the arrangement with Grace, the woman who came to look after Jamie, William and little Jess, was proving such a success. She was calm and capable and the children loved her. Almost her greatest worth was the fact that she was totally flexible when it came to time-keeping. The routine we had fallen into seemed to suit everyone. If Mary was working late, then I was perfectly happy to take Grace's place until she put in an appearance; and if I had to stay on for any reason, Mary never minded keeping Jamie for an extra half-hour. And if we were both late, then Grace, totally unfazed, held the fort until one of us returned.

Paul, too, had a flexible attitude to my working hours. Sometimes he expected me to stay late to finish some particular piece of work, but equally often he told me to go home early if the office was quiet. He was a considerate employer and had a great, self-deprecatory sense of humour, which I appreciated. I didn't at all think of him as the kind of effete Hooray Henry that Sean had described, but I still thought him as weak as water as far as Delia was concerned. Sometimes I wondered, listening to one of her diatribes, if the worm would ever turn. I rather hoped it would, and that I would be there to witness it. But then again, maybe not. There would be blood on the carpet if it ever happened, of that I was certain.

One afternoon, some time towards the end of June, I had finished all the work that was on hand and he sent me home just after three thirty. It had been raining on and off all day and was cold for the time of year.

As I plodded up the valley I contemplated taking advantage of the window of peace and quiet given to me by Jamie's absence at the farm to write the odd letter and perhaps do some ironing, but as I walked I saw that the sky was clearing and a weak sun was at last making its presence felt.

It seemed a sin and a shame to waste the probably short-lived spell of sunshine, for the television forecasters were gloomy about the prospects for the coming week, and it occurred to me that I ought to go and collect Jamie and William and take them down to the beach so that they could let off steam before bedtime.

I had a shrewd suspicion that Grace would welcome the idea, and I wasn't wrong about that, for it had been a difficult day for her. As well as the boys being confined to the house by the rain, thus ensuring all kinds of stir-crazy mischief, baby Jess had been suffering from teething problems; so my offer to take William and Jamie off her hands was enthusiastically accepted.

Once on the beach, they went mad, tearing about with their arms out at right-angles, being aeroplanes. Jamie kept his eye on William as he ran and swooped and banked, just to make sure he was doing it right, for William was his hero, his role model.

I wanted to call out, to tell him to be careful, for the squalls had washed up driftwood and long, shiny ropes of seaweed that could so easily trip or snare the feet of a heedless little boy who wasn't looking where he was going, but I managed to stifle the urge. I didn't want him to turn into a cautious child, frightened of his own shadow – a trap I could see that a lone mother such as I might easily fall into.

We had the beach to ourselves. The tide was a fair way out, which meant that it was possible to go through a kind of archway of rocks which led to a much smaller beach, a sort of annexe to the main stretch of sand. At high tide the gap through the arch was completely filled, and so the smaller beach was cut off and quite inaccessible, unless one was prepared to climb the soaring cliffs which characterised that particular little cove.

My heart sank a little when I saw the way was clear, for I knew at once that the boys would clamour to go and play there. I understood the charm of it, for there were rocks and pools and even caves, which were perfect for hide-and-seek and had been used for this purpose by generation after generation of local children. But it was also easy for younger children to get lost, for some of the caves were longer than others. Despite wanting Jamie to grow up boldly self-sufficient, I had one inflexible rule: he was never to go through to the little beach without me.

At first they were happy swooping around on the main beach and I was hoping they hadn't even noticed the fact that the little cove was accessible. It almost went without saying that, once through there, one or other of them would fall into one of the pools, soaking his trousers and getting chilled to the bone. In spite of the sun, a breeze straight from the Arctic seemed to be sweeping along the coast.

But of course, they didn't stay unaware of it for long. When William began agitating to go through to the little beach – his pleas, inevitably, joined by Jamie's – I tried my best to distract them. The big beach was much better for running, I pointed out. No aeroplane could possibly land on a stony little beach like that one, with all those rocks and pools, and hey – wouldn't it be fun to look for shells down by the water?

'Let's all hold hands and run, run, run,' I enthused.

It didn't work.

'*Please* let me see the lickle fishy,' Jamie begged, referring to all the fascinating rock-pool life that was to be found in that magical place.

'We'll be careful,' William said.

What sort of a spoilsport mother was I?

'OK,' I said. 'We'll go there if you promise not to fall in, and not to go off and hide—'

But they were already running as fast as they could towards the rocky opening and there was little I could do but hurry after them, knowing that as sure as the sun would rise tomorrow, one, if not both, of the boys would be bound to climb the slippery rocks and fall, probably straight into a pool of water. William was such a fearless, adventurous little boy, and where he led, James was sure to go.

The sky was dark again, and the high cliffs seemed to turn it into a cheerless, even menacing place, very different from the cosy little cove it became on a sunny day.

'Just five minutes,' I said, when I caught up with them. 'It's going to rain again soon.'

It's amazing what can happen in five minutes. William fell in a rock pool, as expected, soaking his trousers from ankle to knee, and Jamie measured his length and grazed his forehead. It had become even colder and a large drop of rain splashed on to my hand. Enough, I decided, was enough.

'Come on, boys,' I said briskly. 'Teatime!'

I growled menacingly and pretended to chase them towards the archway and the comparative safety of the main beach. Jamie was happy enough to comply and set off at a great pace, the fall forgotten. However, his high-spirited shouts turned into howls of rage as once more he tripped over a half-buried rock and fell flat on his face.

I ran to him, picked him up and pacified him, thankful to see that he wasn't really hurt. He was just plain mad – which indeed was how I felt myself when I turned round and saw that there was no sign of William. He must have turned round and nipped back through the rocks while I was occupied with Jamie.

The tide had turned and, though it still had some way to go, it wouldn't be too long before the beach was cut off, and William with it.

Picking Jamie up, I retraced my footsteps, only to find when I went through to the beach that it appeared quite empty. Of William, there wasn't a trace.

'William gone,' Jamie informed me.

'So he has,' I said grimly. I put Jamie down and called

William's name, but the wind seemed to fling my voice back in my face and only the gulls replied, shrill and plaintive. The rain was beginning to fall more steadily.

'Wretched child,' I said under my breath, only Jamie's presence preventing my language from being considerably more earthy.

He was hiding, of course – behind the many rocks, in one of the caves. All a big joke, no doubt. I didn't feel like laughing. I called him again, but still there was no response. There were so many hiding places here – but surely he couldn't have gone far in the time? He'd only had a minute or two; but then I knew from experience that that was all a small boy needed to get himself into trouble.

'Come on. We'll have to go and look for him,' I said, and taking Jamie's hand I began looking in the cave nearest to hand.

It was only a shallow one and I needed the nearest glance to see that it was quite empty. My heart sank, for there were others that stretched to several metres, growing narrower and darker as they went along. I kept on calling as I tried the next in line, but still there was no response.

I became aware of a feeling close to panic. Suppose he'd tried to climb the cliffs. Suppose he'd fallen. Suppose I didn't find him before the tide crept up and closed the gap.

Get a grip, I told myself. He can't be far away.

I continued to shout his name as I went into a deeper cave. This was a long, dark one and at the far end water dripped from the roof. There were fissures in the side walls – narrow, but not too narrow for a small boy to hide in. Jamie began to protest and tug at my hand.

'Don't like it, Mummy. Want to go home. Want to go *home*.'

'William,' I called. 'Come on, now. This isn't funny any more.' But only a hollow echo answered me.

'Is this the young man you're looking for?' a voice behind me asked.

I spun round and, to my relief, there was William, held in the arms of a tall, wild-looking, bearded man in an old pair of jeans and a thick fisherman's sweater. He was a total stranger and if he'd had a ring in his ear he would have looked like a picture-book pirate. But I hardly registered his appearance in that moment. He could have been an alien from outer space for all I cared; the fact that my charge was safe was all that mattered. My vivid imagination had conjured pictures of William drowned, or smashed to pieces on the rocks, and I almost sobbed with relief to see that he was not only perfectly well but was, apparently, in the highest of spirits. It was only then that I felt any qualms about the fact that he was in the arms of this wild-looking stranger.

I hurried towards them.

'Oh, William—'

'I hid,' he announced, pleased with himself. He bounced in the wild man's arms. 'I hid ever so much.'

'I know. And I'm very cross,' I said severely.

'I told him you would be,' the man said with a grin, setting him on his feet. 'But he's OK.'

'I'm very grateful to you,' I said. 'I was getting a bit frantic.'

'So I heard.' The unknown man looked slightly amused. 'Boys, I'm afraid, will be boys. However, I rather think you had some time in hand before the tide came in.'

'I know that,' I said, feeling rather ashamed of my panic now that all was well. 'But he's not my child and you do feel so responsible. And William, I shall never, never take you anywhere if you run away from me like that again. It was a very naughty thing to do.'

'She's right, you know,' the man said to William. 'You mustn't do it again.'

Unabashed, William scampered off, out of the cave and through the rocks to the main beach, closely followed by Jamie, with me setting off briskly behind them, not wanting to lose either of them again.

I had the impression that the man was following behind me, but when I looked over my shoulder I saw that he was standing quite still, watching our progress.

'Thanks again,' I called, and he raised his hand in acknowledgement.

Who was he? And where had he come from so suddenly? Had he been there all the time, watching our movements? The thought made me uneasy, even though he had turned out to be a benefactor.

I was pretty sure he wasn't local; I thought I'd detected a slight Northern accent when he spoke. He must, I thought, be a holidaymaker staying in St Venn, who enjoyed a bit of walking and beach-combing. Certainly he wasn't staying at the hotel; he would have stuck out like a sore thumb amid that moneyed, well-groomed clientele. Well, whoever he was and whatever he was doing there, I hoped he wouldn't overestimate the time the tide would take to come in, because I knew from experience that it came in with a rush at the end, always more quickly than you expected.

Once home I phoned Mary, now back from work, to say that I was giving the boys some tea and would bring William home afterwards.

I did so, and accepted her invitation to stay for a moment and have a glass of wine. It was an opportunity to chat, which we hadn't had for some time. I recounted the adventure on the beach, soft-pedalling a bit when it came to William's disobedience, since there's nothing more likely to spoil a friendship than criticism of a friend's children; however, she got the drift and apologised profusely.

'Little wretch,' she said. 'Don't worry – I'll let him know he's been naughty.'

'Go easy – I told him off myself,' I said. 'But I was intrigued by this man who found him. Goodness knows where he came from.'

'I wonder if he's one of the people living in Alf Atkins's cottage,' Mary said. 'You know – that tumbledown place on the cliff towards St Venn. I heard two or three artists had taken it.'

'But it's nearly falling down.'

'Apparently someone came and did it up a bit, just enough to make it habitable. They've been there several weeks, I believe.'

'I hadn't heard. I suppose that's who it could have been. He looked as if he might be an artist.'

'Because he had a beard?' Mary laughed, then sobered at once. 'Like Kit did. Sorry, Prue. I didn't think.'

'Nothing to apologise for.'

'Well, while I'm in a tactless sort of mood,' Mary said, 'why is it that I haven't seen much of my dear brother over this way lately? You two haven't fallen out, have you?'

'No – nothing like that.' I knew I sounded awkward. 'I expect he's busy. And anyway—' I broke off, hesitating a little. 'Anyway, there was never anything romantic between us. He's probably found someone with fewer commitments—'

'Never in a million years. Not if you're talking about Jamie. Ian was crazy about him. Nearly as crazy as he was about you – and still is, as far as I know.'

'Oh, nonsense! There was never anything like that between us. He just helped me out with a few things, that's all.'

'Have it your way.' She didn't pursue the subject, but smiled to herself as if she knew she was right. I thought about Ian, though, as I walked back to the cottage with Jamie. The time had gone by since I'd spoken to him – the whole of the summer, in fact, and there was still no word. Clearly I'd been right to think he'd lost all interest in the reason for Jodie's letter. The trail would surely be stone cold by now.

He must also, I thought, have lost all interest in me. Just as well! It was what I wanted, wasn't it? No commitments, no strings. I'd made that clear enough. It made no sense at all to feel that I'd wilfully thrown away something valuable.

I'd only been back at the cottage a few minutes when Mandy called round. Having been so suspicious of me at first, she had now done a complete U-turn and seemed to regard me more as a kind of agony aunt, a repository for all her secret hopes and fears. This was the latest of many visits; she had walked back to the cottage with me on her free days on several occasions, coming with me to the farm to collect Jamie, highly delighted that he seemed pleased to see her and clutched her hand so readily. She loved children, she told me. She was going to have six – three boys and three girls – when she was married. She couldn't wait.

She was delighted on this occasion to find that she was in time for the bathtime ritual and begged to be allowed to see to Jamie herself. I knew she was competent, and Jamie was amenable, so I was very content to let her get on with it, giving me time to tackle the ironing at last.

I smiled to myself, hearing the laughter from upstairs. Mandy seemed to have a natural talent with children; I felt sorry that she was wasting so much emotion on Sean who, I knew, had absolutely no intention of providing her with the home and family she craved.

Later, with Jamie tucked up in bed, she came down-stairs and had a cup of tea at the kitchen table while I finished the ironing.

'You're very sweet with Jamie,' I said.

'Oh, he's lovely,' she said, looking pleased.

She was, I thought, a sweet girl altogether, though incredibly foolish where Sean was concerned. She talked about him constantly and he could do no wrong in her eyes. Sometimes it had been on the tip of my tongue to tell her his true opinion of her, but I could never find the words. She would have been devastated if she'd known the cruel things he'd said to me.

She had reached for a magazine that had been left on the table and was idly looking through it.

'Look,' she said, holding it up so that I could see a full-page advertisement. 'This chap looks just like Sean, don't he? Some handsome he is.'

'Really?' I said, trying to sound interested. I craned to see it. The advertisement was for aftershave and the young man in question was the object of an adoring beauty with shining blond hair. 'I suppose he does, a bit,' I conceded.

'I reckon Sean could be a model if he wanted to,' she said, continuing to look at the picture in admiration.

'I think he'd rather be a chef,' I said.

'Funny, en't it? A man cooking, I mean. I never knew a man to cook yet, but Sean d'love it. You wouldn't believe it, would you, him growing up with a lord for a grandad and living in a castle and all that. Did he tell you about the castle?'

'Yes, he did.'

'He'm going to take me there,' she confided, smiling up at me. 'He is, honest. Soon's the season's over and we can take a bit of a break, then we'm off to Ireland.' She giggled excitedly. 'I can't believe it – I really, really can't. Me in a castle! Don't say nothing, will you?' she added hastily. 'He told me to keep it quiet.'

'Not a word,' I promised her.

Was now the time to say something? I felt I should, but was at a loss for words. I didn't believe for one minute that Sean had any such intention, but hated to spoil the dream.

In spite of the smile, I suppose my silence must have conveyed some sort of scepticism to Mandy, because she looked at me sharply.

'What's the matter, Prue? Why shouldn't he take me back to his place to meet his grandad?'

His grandad? Surely Sean had said his grandfather was dead and had left no money and that the castle wasn't in the family any more?

Mandy was rushing on. 'Oh, I know back at the hotel in front of everybody he pretends, like, that I'm nothing to him but he says that's because he has to be Professional.' She pronounced the word very carefully, giving each syllable its full weight. 'But he's mad for me, really – can't keep his hands off me, and that's the truth. So why shouldn't he, like, take me back to Ireland? He's told me all about it. There's acres and acres of land, and woods going down to the sea, and, like, servants, and lots of horses in the stables.' She giggled at the thought. 'I hope he doesn't think I'm going to ride one, 'cause I can't do it, no matter what. He can't make me, can he?'

'No. No, I'm sure he wouldn't do that. But Mandy, don't you think—' I hesitated, wondering if I should utter any words of warning.

'Don't I think what?' she asked, on the defensive.

'You don't think that maybe Sean says things he doesn't really mean sometimes – you know, just to please people?' I paused, not knowing how to speak without hurting her. 'That's how he seems to me, anyway.'

'You don't know un like I do. He thinks the world of me!'

'Yes, I'm sure he does,' I lied. 'Oh Mandy, I don't mean to be unkind or to hurt you, really I don't, and I can quite understand why Sean would want to take a pretty girl like you back to his home, but I just have this instinct that he's one of those men who make all kinds of promises they don't really mean to keep. I'd just be a bit careful if I were you. You know – take things with a pinch of salt.'

She sat back in her chair and glared at me, her underlip pushed out like the child she was.

'Honestly, you'm as bad as what Jodie was. She was always going on like that.'

I frowned at her, assimilating this.

'But I thought Sean and Jodie were good friends,' I said.

She gave an incredulous laugh. 'Good friends? Her and Sean? Who told 'ee that?'

'Weren't they?'

'No, they weren't. Never. Couldn't stand each other. Strait-laced, Sean said she was. She might be all smiles on the outside, he said, but inside she'm just like a starchy old maid. Thass the trouble with girls down here, he said. They're all brought up Methodist. So I goes, well I was brought up Chapel, and he goes, you'm different. You'm not a goody-two-shoes like Jodie, always telling other people what they should and shouldn't do.'

'Jodie? Strait-laced?' The idea was so ludicrous, I laughed.

'Well, she was always telling me what to do, anyway. "Don't have nothing to do with un," she says to me. "He'll sweet-talk you into trouble," she said.'

'But Sean *told* me they were good friends.'

'Then he was having 'ee on. Jodie was like someone's old aunt, he said. She didn't like no one to have any fun. Mind you,' she went on, 'I didn't think he was always right about that. Except, like, when she was telling me to leave Sean alone, she was lovely to me. Helped me cut out and sew a dress, and looked after me once when I felt ill and had to go to bed. She was the only one that bothered.'

'But you still didn't think she was right about Sean?'

'No, she wasn't.' There was a stubborn look on Mandy's face. 'He's a lovely chap. Lovely manners, he has. Jodie never had no right to talk about him like she did. Nor you neither,' she added, looking sulky.

'The last thing I want is to hurt you,' I said. 'Just be careful, that's all.'

She left shortly after that, and once I'd put the ironing board away and taken the clothes upstairs, I sat and thought over her puzzling account of Jodie's views on Sean, and his on her, so utterly contradictory to what Sean himself had told me. All this 'closeness' had, as I suspected, been a total lie, contrived just to make me believe that I hadn't been as friendly with Jodie as I imagined.

I was so pleased to think that she had seen right through him, too. Had he tried to make a pass at her, just as he had with me? I could imagine how she would feel about that, having just married Tom.

I should have told Mandy that his grandfather was dead, I thought suddenly. If he could lie to her about that, then he could lie about everything. Even she might be able to see that. Not that I really thought it would have done any good. Mandy was dazzled by him, besotted. I guessed she would have to learn by experience, the same as the rest of us.

And what, I wondered as I threw together a meal for myself, had I learned? Not to trust anyone? Ever? Had I really grown that bitter, that wary of my fellow-men? The thought wasn't a happy one.

Eight

A nother reason I felt grateful for my job was that it had been the cause of my renewing an old friendship with Liz Parnell. We'd been in the same form at St Venn Grammar School and, although we hadn't exactly been bosom pals in the same way that I was with Jodie, we'd always got on well. We even partnered each other in tennis matches and managed to bring home several trophies for the school.

As so often happens, we had somehow lost sight of each other when the time came to leave. We had both gone away from home. She trained as a florist, married an architect and had come back to Cornwall a few years ago to open a flower shop in St Venn. It had been hard going for her at first, but, she told me, getting the contract to do the flowers at Boscothey Manor every week had made a big difference and helped her through the lean times.

'It's my little taste of the high life,' she said to me on one occasion. 'I enjoy it.'

'Even with Delia on your back?'

She laughed at that. She was an easygoing kind of person with a round, good-humoured face that seemed as if it were about to break into a smile even when she was engrossed in the most elaborate flower arrangement – which, naturally, was what Delia demanded. Her taste ran to huge urns with a vast quantity of flowers and foliage arranged in the manner of Constance Spry – which, I suppose, were more suited to the dimensions of Boscothey Manor than the minimalist designs that Liz usually favoured. I had often heard Delia barking at her from a distance, giving her instructions in her own peculiarly aggressive way. Liz was excellent at her job and needed no instruction from anyone, but Delia was not the kind of person who could bear to efface herself.

That Thursday afternoon in mid-September was no exception. Liz had come into the office after she had finished her work, to collect the mail. On her days for coming to the hotel, it was her usual custom to take the day's post with her when she left and post it at the main post office in St Venn, thus saving one of the other staff – usually Benny – the drive. Trenellack was nearer and was the proud possessor of one postbox, but the last collection there was at 3.30 in the afternoon, so St Venn was the better option.

I had handed the letters over and we were just exchanging a few friendly words when Delia marched in and informed Liz that she wasn't satisfied with the main flower arrangement in the hall.

'There's something quite bizarre about it,' she said. 'Yes – *bizarre!* I can't put my finger on it, but I think it needs to be wider in some way.'

'Wider?' Liz looked rather baffled. 'Let's go and see it and you can show me what's wrong.'

She put the letters down again and went out with Delia, casting a speaking glance in my direction. In five minutes she was back.

'All seems well now,' she said.

'What did you do?'

'I moved one piece of foliage slightly to the left and put in two extra lilies. And now, apparently, it's perfectly acceptable. Not bizarre at all.'

'How do you put up with it?'

'It's impossible to argue with Delia. You should know that by now. I just smile and agree with whatever she suggests, then do exactly what I want.'

'Well, I'm glad you've sorted the flowers out,' I said. 'We don't do bizarre at Boscothey Manor, you know.'

She laughed, picked up the letters, said she would see me next week, and left.

It occurred to me that Paul, in his dealings with his wife, had developed much the same strategy as Liz. Like her, he had learned that arguing did no good at all – which was, I reflected, the entire problem. Everyone gave in to her for the sake of a quiet life.

At this point, Paul breezed into the office.

'Has Liz gone?' he asked.

'Just this minute.'

'Damnit, I was hoping to catch her. I meant to put this letter with the others.'

'I don't think she's left the yard,' I said, peering out of the window. 'Oh yes – there she goes.'

'Never mind. It's not really urgent.' He reached into an inner pocket, took out an envelope and threw it into my out-tray before going into his inner sanctum. 'Tomorrow will do.' He carried on towards his office before turning back. 'By the way,' he said. 'Delia's off to London for a few days next Wednesday. You know how it is: people to meet, shows to see, shops to be plundered. You'd better note it down in the diary.'

'Right. When do you expect her back?'

'Sunday.'

I made the entry then and there, then continued with the letter I was writing. Another big wedding was in prospect and the bride's mother had written giving instructions concerning every aspect of it – but something was disturbing me, nagging at my consciousness, begging for recognition. What was it?

I pushed it to the back of my mind. I had to finish this letter. Even so, before I got to the last paragraph, a thought struck me.

If Jodie had printed that letter out intending to post it, she had two obvious choices in front of her. She could either have put it with the hotel mail, in which case, being a Thursday, Liz would have taken it to St Venn Post Office; or Jodie could have taken it herself to post in Trenellack, where it would have lain in the box until the following morning. This seemed unlikely, as she was clearly anxious that it should reach Ian as quickly as possible.

There was, of course, a third alternative: she could have intended to drive into St Venn herself and post it after work. But apparently she had done no such thing. In fact she had done none of the above. The letter, it seemed, had never gone anywhere.

Which made no sense at all to me, and never had from the moment I had read it. Urgency was expressed in every line of that letter and, as she said herself, she desperately needed advice. I still wondered why she hadn't faxed it; maybe the machine had been on the blink. Paul had bought a new one shortly after I'd joined the hotel, which seemed to indicate the old one wasn't very reliable.

In any case, if the letter went by first-class post that afternoon, it should have arrived on Ian's desk first thing the following morning. I felt she was justified in assuming that would be soon enough. I just knew for certain that she'd intended that letter to reach him, one way or another.

So back to the only other alternative. The letter had somehow been intercepted before it was posted. Mentally I went through the Thursday-afternoon routine: Liz would have come into the office, just as she did today. She'd probably have had a few moments' chat with Jodie, picked up the mail and taken it to St Venn, where she would have had no reason not to put it in the box along with all the other letters. She wouldn't even have known that it wasn't a run-of-the-mill communication from the hotel, for no doubt the envelope would have been the standard hotel issue, the address typed like all the others.

The answer hit me so hard that I gasped, and, just as with other sudden revelations, I couldn't imagine why I hadn't thought of it before. For six months the answer had been there, staring me in the face, and yet it was only now that I realised it.

There was one thing on the calendar for that particular Thursday in March that was so ordinary and mundane that I had completely disregarded it: Delia's dental appointment at 4.45. She had gone into town that afternoon and could easily have taken the mail with her instead of leaving it to Liz to take a little later. And it would be totally out of character for her not to have leafed through the envelopes to see that Paul hadn't left anything undone. Or done anything he ought not to have done, maybe.

She would have seen the envelope addressed to Ian Channing, of Channing, Lowther & Partners of Truro. Even if she didn't know Ian Channing personally, she would have recognised the name of the firm as being that of a firm of solicitors, and she must have wondered what business Paul had with them. Did she imagine that the worm had, indeed, turned and that he was contemplating divorce? Or was it simply sheer curiosity on her part?

We all had good reason to know that Delia hated not to be in control of the tiniest, most insignificant detail. I had not the smallest doubt that she would have opened the letter if she'd found it; but then, Jodie would have known that too. There was no way she would have wanted Delia to get her hands on it, even if it was semi-concealed among the other envelopes waiting for the post.

So did my theory fall to the ground? Not necessarily, I thought. There were a hundred reasons why Delia could have called in to see Paul before leaving for the dentist. The letters might have been ready and waiting for Liz on Jodie's desk when she swept through the office and picked them up in passing. Jodie would only have been able to watch helplessly, hoping against hope that her letter would pass without notice; a vain hope, as she must have guessed. On the other hand, she could have been out of the office for a moment or two. Gone to the kitchen for a cup of tea, perhaps. It was something I often did, between three thirty and four.

This, I felt, was something I had to tell Ian, even if he dismissed it as pure supposition. There had been a number of times during the summer when I had hovered over the phone, wondering whether I should give him a ring, ask him over, remind him of my existence. I had always drawn back, however. He knew where I was if he wanted to find me.

He'd been on a sailing holiday with some friends round the Greek islands, I'd heard from Mary. He'd had a wonderful time, apparently, and developed an amazing tan. I wanted to ask her if the friends had included any special girl, but I kept my mouth shut. She might think that I was really concerned about his love life – and of course I wasn't. It meant nothing to me. I just wanted him to be happy.

Still, I missed him and was interested in his welfare. Couldn't he see that? I'd never said that I wanted to lose touch with him.

So I was glad that I had a good reason to contact him and I did so the moment I got home, knowing that he would still be in the office. I must have caught Glenys in a good mood because I was put through straight away.

'Hi,' he said. 'How are you, Prue? It's good to hear

from you – but you know, this is really strange. Must be extra-sensory perception, or something. I was going to ring you tonight.'

'Really?' I felt I had every right to sound sceptical. I'd lost count of the number of weeks that had passed since the last time we'd spoken.

'Yes, really. I have some news. Is it OK if I drop over this evening – say about seven?'

'Yes, of course. But can't you tell me—'

'I'd rather not. I'll see you later.'

'Wait – I've got some news, too. I've just realised that Delia might have been able to see the letter Jodie wrote to you before it was posted. It's highly likely she took it to St Venn herself. Not that Jodie meant her to, of course.'

There was a short silence from Ian's end.

'Well – good for you,' he said, with what I detected was a note of reluctance in his voice. 'We'll talk about it later.'

Maybe he was busy, I thought as I put the phone down. Maybe someone had come into the room. Never mind – we would be seeing each other that evening, and I found the thought a particularly cheering one. What a good thing that I'd splashed out on a decent bottle of wine the last time I went to the supermarket, for just such an occasion as this!

He arrived dead on seven. I felt suddenly shy when I saw his car draw up outside the cottage, the memory of our last conversation all those months ago on the beach returning to embarrass me. Why had I been so prickly – so unable to meet the poor guy halfway, or even be the slightest bit kind to him? He hadn't deserved such a terse rejection.

His greeting, I thought, was a little wary as I opened the door to him, but Jamie, already in his pyjamas, broke the ice by rushing to meet him and clutching him round the knees, just as if he'd never been away.

'Eem, Eem, I've got a new fire engine. Come and see!'

'Hi, mate – good to see you!' Ian picked him up and held him high. 'How've you been?'

'The *fire* engine! Come and see.'

'You show me,' Ian said, setting him down on his feet.

They went into the living room together, leaving me to follow behind, enjoying the look of them – so much at ease with each other, so happy to be together again.

There was, of course, no opportunity to talk about anything serious while Jamie was about, but eventually he allowed Ian to tuck him into bed and the two of us were at last alone.

I poured him a glass of wine as he joined me in the kitchen.

'You first,' I said, handing it to him. 'What have you got to tell me?'

He took the glass and held it without drinking, looking at me with a thoughtful, even sombre look in his eyes.

'We've traced Kit,' he said. 'He's in Spain.'

'Oh!' I took a quick gulp of my wine. 'The Costa del Crime, I imagine.'

'No. He's in a place called Cadaqués, not far from the French border, shacked up with a dancer.'

'I'm sorry for her,' I said after a moment. 'How did you find him?'

'We have people who do that sort of thing. Track people down. I –' he hesitated – 'I wondered if you still wanted us to serve divorce papers.'

I turned and looked up at him wide-eyed.

'Of course I do! How could you possibly think I wouldn't? The sooner the better as far as I'm concerned.'

'You're not going to be able to get any money out of him. It seems he's on his uppers, living on what the girl earns.'

'Now why doesn't that surprise me?' I sat down at

the table, took another sip. 'Look, Ian,' I said, as he came and joined me at the table. 'I don't want or expect any money, even though the bastard owes me. And, thank heaven, I can manage to cover any costs myself now. I just want to get shot of him – before he takes it into his head to come back and mess up Jamie's life, just like he messed up mine. Not,' I added, 'that he's ever shown the slightest interest in his son.'

'Apparently his girlfriend's pregnant. She'll have to give up the act soon.'

I thought this over.

'Then I'm really, really sorry for her,' I said at last, 'because he'll leave her. I just know it. And if he's desperate for cash, he might come back here to see what else he can get out of me.'

'We'll get on with serving the papers at once,' Ian said. 'It shouldn't take long.'

'And Ian, please make sure he has no access to Jamie. Oh, I know all about fathers' rights, but Kit forfeited them ages ago. Any influence from him can only be bad. Fortunately, I don't think he'll care.'

Ian looked at me for a moment without speaking.

'Don't be too vengeful,' he said at last. 'One day Jamie might want to know his father.'

'Over my dead body!'

'People change, Prue. Do things they regret. Oh, heaven knows I understand why you don't want him coming and going as he pleases, but I honestly think, for Jamie's sake—' He stopped right there, as if he could see that he wasn't getting anywhere with me. 'Well, let's not bother about that right now. The important thing is, we've found him and now we can get on with the divorce.'

'Right,' I said.

'Don't worry about anything – not the fees or anything

else. We'll talk about all that later . . . you have enough to cope with right now.'

He never spoke a truer word. I felt dazed and almost incapable of taking in the facts. I don't think I realised until that moment how the memory of my life with Kit had shadowed and burdened me, and I needed, for a second, to draw breath and readjust.

Ian reached to pour some more wine into my depleted glass.

'Don't worry,' he said again. 'It'll be OK. You can leave everything to me.'

'That must be the most comforting sentence in the whole of the English language,' I said.

'Well, I mean it. I'll deal with it right away.'

'Thanks.' For a second I hesitated, thinking this brief word of appreciation totally inadequate. I should kiss him, I thought. Just a peck on the cheek to show I'm really grateful.

I didn't do it, though, and merely flicked a small, strained smile in his direction. I knew he would do his best for me; knew, inside me, that ultimately I would admit he was right about keeping a chink of the door open so that Jamie might one day know his father. The main consideration was that I was about to be truly free. Sometimes it had seemed that this was a moment that would never come.

'Believe me,' I said at last, 'I'm very grateful. I kind of thought you'd forgotten all about me and my affairs.'

'Well, you did me an injustice. I never forgot you for a moment.' He was serious, not making a joke of it.

'I can see that now. I'm sorry. And truly thankful.'

He smiled then. 'All part of the service.'

We raised our glasses and clinked them together, the atmosphere suddenly lightened.

'I can't believe it,' I said. 'He won't fight it, will he?'

'He can't, Prue.'

He told me more about how the firm intended to proceed, but at last I remembered my theory regarding Jodie's letter.

'What do you think about it?' I asked him.

'That Delia could have intercepted it?'

'Yes. She could have done, Ian. So easily. She went into St Venn to the dentist that afternoon and could well have taken the mail. I can't imagine why I didn't think of it before.'

'Surely the last thing Jodie would have done would be to give it to her to take to the post?'

'Of course not – she wouldn't have meant that to happen. But Liz – you know, the florist – usually takes the post on a Thursday and Jodie could easily have put hers in the pile with the others. Liz wouldn't have known the difference, or cared if she did.'

'So why didn't Liz take it?'

'I don't know. How could I know? I'm just saying how it could have happened. Delia went into St Venn that afternoon and if she'd gone into the office for a second first, she might easily have swept the letters up and taken off before Jodie could say a word. It's the way she does things, Ian. She's always quick and decisive and I've seen it happen before. I can always check with Liz. She might possibly remember.'

'No,' he said, putting down his glass on the table beside him. 'No, don't do that.'

'Why not?'

'Because I really don't think you ought to involve yourself in any of this business. Will you promise me?'

'Like hell!' I said indignantly, sitting up very straight. 'Just because everyone else has forgotten that Jodie might have been killed—'

'Don't be daft,' Ian said, interrupting my rant. 'No

one's forgotten anything. I happen to know that there's an on-going investigation and it's almost in its final stages. Any interference by you or me or anyone else could ruin it. Not to mention that it might put you in danger.'

'Investigation?' I seized on that one word and asked the question derisively. 'What investigation? No one's been near the hotel to find out what went on that day. No sign of the police, no statements taken. What kind of an investigation is that?'

'An undercover one, you idiot,' Ian said, but gently. 'One that's been going on for weeks. Months, even. And one that could be blown if anyone talks out of turn or gives anyone at Boscothey any idea of what's going on. That, partly at any rate, is why I've kept well clear of you the whole of the summer – with difficulty, I may add. I was afraid that I'd give something away without meaning to, and that you'd then give something away at the hotel without meaning to—'

I felt distinctly outraged at this.

'It didn't occur to you that if I'd known what was going on I'd have been the soul of discretion? I'm perfectly capable of keeping my mouth shut, you know.'

'I don't doubt it. I was just following instructions – and, be fair, accidents can happen. You can't let slip any information if you've never heard it in the first place. And after all – look what happened to Jodie. She let it be known that she knew something was going on.'

'So – so they think she really was murdered?'

'Yes, they do.'

'By Delia?'

'Not necessarily. She's not alone in this.'

'Does Tom know?'

'Yes.'

'Oh well,' I said sarcastically. 'He's a man, of course.

He can be told, but not me because we all know that women talk.'

'Tom's not here to be in any danger and you weren't told anything because you're there, on the spot. In the lion's den, if you like. The less you know, the better for you. You must see that.'

I thought this over and, reluctantly, conceded his point.

'I suppose you're right,' I said. 'But it's not much good telling me not to get involved, because I've been involved right from the beginning. Can't you tell me what's going on?'

'Oh, Prue! It's not that I don't want to, or don't trust you—'

'I know, I know! You're acting under instructions. Well, I'm not daft, you know, and I can have my theories as well as the next man. Suppose I tell you what I think?' I leaned forward, looking into his face. 'I think that Boscothey Manor is being used for smuggling – drugs, I suppose. What else? Time was when it was brandy for the parson, baccy for the clerk.'

'"And watch the wall, my darling, while the gentlemen go by."'

'Exactly. Only they're not gentlemen any more, if they ever were, and anyone can buy those things on a booze cruise to France so they're not worth the time and effort. I'm right, aren't I? It's a perfect situation, after all, with that rocky little cove only feet away from it. A boat could easily come in there at dead of night, if the tide's right. Go on,' I jeered in the face of his silence. 'Now tell me I'm wrong.'

He laughed, a touch ruefully.

'No, you're not wrong,' he said. 'But I still don't feel free to tell you the whole lot. Let's say I'll seek further instructions.'

'You're the most maddening man.'

'I gave them my word I'd keep it all to myself.'

'Who's "them"? Where are they hiding?'

'There are two men and a girl, living in Alf Atkins's old cottage on the cliff. They've been passing themselves off as artists – the girl is actually pretty good – but in fact they've had the whole place under surveillance for months.'

Light dawned.

'The man on the beach!' I said. 'I saw one of them, when I took the two boys down once. William went and hid in a cave and this chap with a beard suddenly appeared from nowhere.'

'That sounds like Max.'

'What I don't understand,' I said, after thinking this over for a few moments, 'is why Jodie wrote to you and didn't go straight to the police, if she found out about all of this.'

Ian shrugged his shoulders.

'Maybe she simply wasn't sure,' he said. 'She might have thought that alerting the police would mean they'd be swarming all over the hotel, and that if by any chance she were wrong she'd lose her job. Maybe she thought that if she brought me in as a middleman, she'd be able to keep out of it.'

'She'd be anxious not to ruin the hotel's reputation unfairly,' I pointed out. 'I can't tell you how we're all pressurised into avoiding that.'

Ian gave a grunt of laughter.

'And yet the Ransleighs are running the biggest smuggling operation seen for years! A strange and dangerous way to promote the hotel's interests, wouldn't you say?'

'You think they're both involved?'

'Oh, yes.'

Yes, of course. I remembered Paul's trip to London, the day after the one marked on the calendar. I felt sorry about that. I didn't like to think that Paul was as bad as Delia. And surely – *surely* – he couldn't have been the one who killed Jodie? I looked at Ian in horror.

'You mean one of them could have pushed Jodie—'

'Not necessarily. And that,' he said with mock severity, 'is absolutely all I'm going to say on the matter, so let's talk about something else.'

'Those numbers in the diary,' I said. 'They were times of high tides, weren't they? It's only just occurred to me.'

'No comment,' Ian said. 'And shall I tell you what's just occurred to me? Why don't I nip to St Venn for an Indian?'

I relaxed a little and smiled at him. I wouldn't try to ferret out any more information, I decided. It wasn't really fair on a man like Ian, whose word was his bond. Instead, I'd just sit back and enjoy having someone else take charge.

It was a novel experience, being looked after by a man of integrity. I could, I thought, get used to it quite easily. And he did have lovely eyes.

Nine

After Ian left to pick up the takeaway, I put plates to warm and set places at the table. He'd only been gone about twenty minutes when the telephone rang and I discovered he was at the other end of it.

'I'm at Alf Atkins's cottage,' he said. 'I was about to pass it on the way to St Venn when it occurred to me that it might be a good idea to let them know you were in the picture.'

'What?' I was amused at this. 'I'd say I was still pretty much in the dark!'

'Well, semi in the picture,' he corrected himself. 'Anyway, they think that maybe now's the time to let you know the rest, so Max has suggested coming over later this evening to fill you in. Thought I'd better check to see if that's all right with you.'

'Nothing I'd like better,' I said. 'And about time too, if I may say so.'

More than anything, I wanted to know what was going on and who was involved, though the more I thought about it, the more I understood why they'd kept me out of things until that point. Knowing that either Delia or Paul could have been responsible for Jodie's death would have made it very difficult for me to go on working at the hotel. It would be hard enough from now on, until things were settled one way or the other.

Eventually Ian came back and we ate our supper,

deliberately talking about other things. His holiday, mutual friends, a recent play on TV. It was an almost tangible relief, however, when a knock heralded Max's arrival. There really was room for only one subject in my mind at that moment.

I went to open the door to the man I had already seen on the beach.

'Ah, the agitated lady,' he said, smiling and holding out his hand to shake mine as he came into the cottage.

'The wild man of the caves! You're very welcome. As you know,' I said, 'you already have my undying gratitude for rescuing young William.'

'I hope he's learned the error of his ways.'

'So do I – but somehow I doubt it! Come on into the sitting room. You're just in time for coffee – and please, do sit down. And you, Ian,' I added, as he greeted Max. The entire cottage seemed far too small to hold these two large men comfortably.

'I'm sure you're anxious to know what's going on, so I'll cut to the chase,' Max said, having taken a seat.

'Just hang on one second while I get the coffee, and then you can tell me everything.'

I went to the kitchen but was back in a moment with the tray. 'Now fire away,' I said when they both had mugs in their hands.

'Well, now—' Max paused for a moment. Censoring the narrative, I wondered? Choosing what to tell me and what to keep to himself? I couldn't help wondering if I were really about to learn the whole story, even now. He looked at me and smiled, as if he knew exactly what I was thinking. 'As you know, I'm Max – DS Max Taylor, if we're being formal. Drug Squad. We've always been interested in this particular part of the coast. There are so many small coves and inlets, and as everyone knows, historically they were always infamous for the smuggling trade. I know I don't need to give you a history lesson.

'Things aren't so very different now. We already had this area under surveillance, and when word came about your friend's death and the suspicions she'd hinted at only just a few days before, we felt that the chances were it was no coincidence. The hotel's ideally placed, after all.'

'Do you know what made Jodie suspicious?' I asked.

'Not precisely, no. Maybe she overheard something.'

'And this was enough to make someone push her over the cliff?'

'She put her suspicions in writing.'

'But she didn't specify—'

'She didn't have to.'

'The coroner seemed to think it was an accident.'

'He didn't have all the facts.'

'Then who did it?'

'It could have been any of them, but I have my suspicions.'

I looked at him expectantly, but he said no more.

'Delia could have known about the letter,' I said. 'I explained to Ian how she could have read it.'

'I know,' Max said. 'He told me. It could have happened that way. Certainly someone found out that Jodie thought something illegal was going on, it doesn't really matter how, and that was why she had to die. As I said before, the person who actually carried out the murder could have been one of several people. It could even have been someone who found that letter on the computer, just as you did, though admittedly that doesn't explain why Ian didn't get it. What you must realise, Mrs Ryder – may I call you Prue? – is that they're all playing for high stakes. We're talking megabucks here.'

'Haven't you got enough evidence to arrest them?'

'We need more. We think we know who's at the London end, but we want to catch them red-handed.'

'How do you propose to do that?'

'Well now—' He looked at me for a moment without speaking and I somehow knew instinctively that he was about to ask me to do something; something that, judging from his expression, he guessed I wouldn't want to do. Ian spoke for the first time.

'Max, I honestly don't think Prue ought to get mixed up in this,' he said. 'The more I think about it, the less I like it.'

'Ssh, Ian,' I said. 'Let Max tell me what he wants.'

'We really could do with your help,' Max said. 'We've discovered from our opposite numbers in France that a delivery's going to be made next week, possibly Wednesday, maybe Thursday, which means that either Mr or Mrs Ransleigh will be going to London the day after—'

'Thursday,' I said. 'It's Delia and that's when she's going to London. Paul told me today.'

Max's eyes gleamed.

'So Wednesday's the night. Excellent.'

'And you'll arrest them then?'

'Not exactly. Oh, Customs and Excise will have a man on shore and a cutter close by so they can follow them and pick up the crew after they've dumped their cargo – making sure there's plenty of photographic evidence of the handover, of course. But we don't want to alert the Ransleighs. We want to follow the car to its destination in London – which is where we need your help. We need to know which car she'll be driving. Once we know that, we can bug it and see where it goes. Then we'll have them. All of them.'

I thought this over for a second. It didn't seem a particularly difficult task.

'OK,' I said, quite readily. 'I'll try.'

'Don't, for the love of heaven, put yourself in any

danger. That's the last thing we want. We just felt that as Paul Ransleigh's secretary you'd be in a position to get this information in general conversation, without arousing suspicion.'

I nodded. 'I don't see why not. I'm not sure how I'll do it, but it'll come to me.'

'I don't like it,' Ian said. 'We've kept her out of it until now. Suppose someone at the hotel gets wind of the fact that Prue's suspicious . . .'

He sounded angry, as if he were seriously concerned on my behalf, and though I felt he was worrying unduly, I couldn't help feeling warmed by it. It seemed a very long time since anyone had been quite so concerned about me.

'It's all right, Ian,' I said softly. 'Really. It'll be easy.'

'Don't underestimate them, that's all,' he said. 'Remember what they did to Jodie.'

I turned to Max.

'Will you be able to find out who killed her?'

'I certainly hope so.'

'I can't imagine it can have been Paul. He's a gentle sort of soul. Rather a sweetie, really. And Delia – well, I don't particularly like her. She's vain and snobbish and manipulative, but I can't see her murdering anyone. They were both so *sorry* about Jodie. I can't believe it was all a sham.'

'They are both criminals,' Max pointed out. 'With a lot to lose. And, as I said before, there are others involved.'

'Others at the hotel? Like, who?'

'The chef,' Max said. 'The French one.'

'Oh, of course!' I was remembering what Sean had told me – or half told me – about Gaston. 'He's been in trouble with the police before, hasn't he?'

'Several times,' Max said. 'But he's always managed to wriggle out of it. This time we're going to make it stick.'

'Look,' Ian said, 'I'm sorry to bang on about this. I know how important it is. It's just that I think it puts Prue in a horribly dangerous situation. After all, we all know what happened to Jodie at the merest whisper of suspicion.'

'Oh Ian, do stop fussing,' I said. 'Lighten up! I'm sure I can find out about the car without any trouble. As Max says, I can raise it in general conversation. Believe me, I can exercise tact when I try.'

He said no more on the subject, though I could see from his expression that he was no happier. Later he relaxed a little as the three of us continued to talk, straying far from the events at Boscothey Manor. Max, it seemed, had fallen in love with this stretch of coastline and was determined to bring his wife and family to stay here the following year.

It was dark when he left. Ian came with me to the door to see him off, and for a moment we stood looking out into the night after the car had driven away. There was a hint of an autumnal nip in the air but it was clear and bright, a million stars shining in the unpolluted air of the bay.

'Nice night,' I said.

He looked at me without speaking and when we both stepped back into the lighted kitchen I could see that the sombre look was back on his face.

'Prue—'

'Don't look so worried, Ian,' I said. 'It's going to be all right. Come on, there's another dreg in the bottle. We might as well finish it.'

I went past him, with the intention of picking up the bottle from the kitchen table, but before I could reach for it he turned me round to face him, his hands on my shoulders.

'It's no use telling me not to worry,' he said. 'I don't

seem to be able to help it. Maybe it's because this plan of Max's renders totally pointless all the efforts I made to stay away from you this summer. I didn't want anyone to be able to make any connection between you and whatever was going on. I made Max swear to keep you out of it.'

'Ian.' The full impact of this was dawning on me slowly. 'Was that the real reason you stayed away from me? It wasn't from choice?'

'Of course it wasn't!'

'You could have explained!'

'Maybe I was over-cautious – but if I'd explained properly, it could have made life very difficult for you at Boscothey. You would have had to carry on as normal, knowing all the time that the Ransleighs were suspected of God-knows-what. This seemed by far the best way.'

'I thought I'd offended you and you were never going to speak to me again.'

'Why would you think that?'

I stared at him, astonished that he seemed not to have worked that out for himself.

'Well, it's obvious, isn't it? That day on the beach when I was so horrible—'

'You *weren't* horrible! It was all my fault! I spoke out of turn. I knew you weren't ready to make any commitment, to me or anyone else. I knew I ought to be patient. It was just that everything had been so great that day that I thought – I thought, What the hell, let's go for it! God knows, sometimes I felt I'd been biding my time for ever. I wanted you so much, Prue.'

I remembered that strange moment when my whole body had seemed to hunger for him, and how frightened I'd been, partly by my own emotions and partly by his. Had we both been longing for each other at one and the same time? What idiots, I thought. What total idiots! Well,

I couldn't speak for Ian, but I'd paid for it. It had been a lonely summer.

'I was one crazy, mixed-up bird-brain,' I said. 'The last thing I wanted to do was hurt you. I've missed you so much all this time.'

'Honestly?' He looked as if he couldn't believe his ears.

'Of course I did. And so did Jamie.'

'Oh.' He drew back a little and crooked an eyebrow at me. 'Well, I know I'm the world's expert on sandcastles, but I rather hoped your kind of missing was a little different from his.'

I laughed at that and reached to put my hand against his face, rubbing it gently with the back of my knuckles. It occurred to me that, while Kit was handsome and Sean positively dazzling, Ian's looks were the sort that would go on getting better as he grew in confidence and wisdom and humour. How could I ever have thought him ordinary?

'I think it was on a different sort of scale,' I said. 'Possibly.'

'Oh God, Prue!' It was almost a groan, and suddenly his arms were round me and I was being held tight against his shoulder. I could feel the hardness of the bone, smell the scent of his skin, feel his lips against my hair. And I had no wish to pull away; none whatsoever. It simply felt right and inevitable and as if I had always belonged there.

I lifted my head and we kissed, quite tentatively at first, then breathlessly, with increasing passion, murmuring our want and our need for each other. There was laughter, too, with a breathless edge to it, and excitement as I pulled him towards the steep little staircase. No time now to think that I was the girl who had sworn off men for ever. I had changed, recovered from Kit, recovered from the hurt, and I was ready to get on with my life.

The night was paling towards dawn when Ian, very

reluctantly, left me. We'd both agreed that maybe it wouldn't be right for Jamie to find him in my bed at this early stage in our changed relationship, but it was hard to part, even though, as it was a Saturday, we knew that we could meet again before many hours had passed. He had a date to play squash with a friend quite early, but would be back again well before lunch. I slept on a little, still drunk with happiness and fulfilment, not giving more than a passing thought to the task that Max had set me.

On Monday I found that another clear night had given way to a pale, misty morning. What a difference a week-end could make, I reflected as I dressed for work – and I wasn't thinking about the weather. I was thinking about Ian and the hours we had spent together over the past couple of days. Not doing much: just ordinary things, like a bit of clearing up in the garden and shopping and a walk down to the beach. Jamie, of course, was in his seventh heaven having Ian to play with again, and as for me – well, if there were an eighth heaven, that's where you'd find me. From time to time we'd exchange glances, laugh at nothing, reach to hold a hand. I found it astonishing that I was capable of feeling this way again.

We agreed, very sensibly, that Ian should go back to his own house on Sunday night, but somehow it didn't turn out that way and a new day was beginning to break when he finally left, still begging me to be careful what I said when trying to elicit the information Max needed.

'Trust me,' I said. 'And don't worry so much.'

Mary hadn't left for work when I went up to the farm to leave Jamie the next morning. She was busy putting clothes into the washing machine when I went through the kitchen door, but I immediately detected an air of suppressed excitement about her as she straightened up to grin widely at me.

'Well, hello,' she said. 'And how are you today?'

'Fine,' I said warily, somehow knowing that the question wasn't as straightforward as it appeared.

'Good night?'

'Excellent, thank you.'

She burst out laughing.

'Who's as sly as a snake, then? You can't fool me, Prue Ryder. My brother was at your house *all night*! Don't attempt to deny it.'

'My God,' I said, throwing up my hands. 'This place has always been the same! Sneeze in a curtained room and the whole village knows you've got a cold.'

'Ain't it the truth?' Mary said. 'But you can level with me. Honestly, I couldn't be more pleased.'

'How do you know?' I asked.

She laughed and went back to stuffing the washing machine.

'Saw the car. Roger's Aunt Ida and Uncle George were celebrating their golden wedding and we didn't get back until two in the morning. Oh, Prue, I'm really glad you two have got it together. You're made for each other.'

'Maybe,' I said, attempting to be cool. I couldn't keep it up, however, and I knew my beaming smile instantly gave away any secrets I might want to keep.

Mary straightened up and came over to give me a hug.

'He's a lucky guy,' she said. 'But then, he's not such a bad chap, either. Honestly, I couldn't be more pleased.'

'It's early days,' I cautioned her. 'Don't go running away with the idea we're about to tie the knot.'

She gave an omniscient smile.

'Want to bet?' she said.

That there were choices ahead I didn't doubt, but I wasn't worried by them that morning and there was a spring in my step as I walked the field path to the hotel. It was only as I got closer that I recognised that I was beginning, after all, to feel a little nervous. On the face of it, it should prove quite easy to find out what vehicle Delia would choose for her trip to London, but clearly it was an important step in the investigation and I had to be careful not to give anything away. After Jodie, I could see why any of the people involved might be sensitive about direct questions.

Once in my office, I plunged into completing the wedding arrangements I had been working on before the weekend, and I took a fair amount of dictation from Paul, not allowing the thought of his criminal activities to enter my head. It was, indeed, easy to forget them, if only temporarily, for he was his usual drily amusing self. It was going to be very hard for me ever to believe he had anything to do with Jodie's death.

Delia swished in and out of the office early on, but then disappeared about her duties elsewhere; I didn't see her again until after lunch. Then, while I was in the kitchen having my afternoon cup of tea with Isobel, she came and joined us, clearly in an unusually relaxed and friendly mood.

'Isn't it wonderful when things quieten down?' she said, stretching her legs and settling comfortably into a chair. 'It's just heaven having a little time to breathe. Not that I'm complaining,' she added quickly. 'The more guests the merrier as far as I'm concerned – yes, thank you, Sean. You can bring my tea over here. Still,' she went on, 'I'm ready for a rest.'

'I think we all are,' Isobel said, a little chippily.

Delia looked at her coldly.

'We all work hard during the summer, Isobel,' she said. 'I acknowledge that and appreciate it. But it's the responsibility that's so wearing. I don't think you others realise how I'm forced to live, think and breathe this hotel, twenty-four hours a day, seven days a week.'

'You should get away for a rest,' I said craftily.

She smiled at me.

'As it happens, I'm doing just that. I'm going to London next Thursday. You know, Prue, I'm surprised you don't go up sometimes yourself. With your background you must be starved of culture.'

I murmured something about my little boy, but she ignored such considerations.

'There are some wonderful art exhibitions on at the moment,' she said. 'I know you'd be interested in them, particularly the Victorian watercolours at the Royal Academy. I'm going with a friend next Friday.'

'How lovely!' I made my voice casual, and went on sipping my tea. 'I really envy you. Does this mean you'd like me to book you a seat on the train?'

'Lord, no!' Delia brushed away this idea with a laugh. 'I'll drive up. I always do. It only takes about four and a half hours in the Saab. I should be there at lunchtime if I leave at a reasonable time.'

'Lucky you,' I said lightly. 'I can't remember the last time I was in London.'

What I really meant was: lucky me, for I could hardly believe that the information I wanted had been dropped in my lap so easily, without any risk of discovery at all.

Ian was even more delighted than I when I reported back to him that evening.

'Thank God for that,' he said in heartfelt tones. 'That's your part done. It's over to the professionals now. They'll do what's necessary.'

'I wonder what will happen at the hotel?'

'A complete change of staff, that's for sure.'

'The job suits me so well.'

'Mm.' He looked at me reflectively. 'There's no reason why you should have to leave, is there? But I guess there'll be a whole lot of changes for us to think about, one way and another. Like finding a place that's big enough for the three of us.'

When I didn't speak, he looked at me with a slight frown and an element of anxiety in his eyes, as if, perhaps, he had gone too far too quickly and was fearful of my reaction. And for a moment I was fearful, too. I felt a faint, residual breath of panic, as if the past still threw a faint shadow over me.

'We'll talk about it,' I said. 'Let's not rush things.'

'No pressure,' he said. 'Just something to bear in mind.'

We continued to look into each other's eyes for a long moment and I found myself relaxing. It would happen. Maybe not quite yet, but before too long. What was between us, I suddenly knew without doubt, was something that would last and grow and strengthen us all our days. Desire was a part of it – a big part of it – but it was nothing like the blind, self-deluding passion I'd felt for Kit which had all the substance of Cornish mist.

The hotel was strangely quiet and Paul sent me off early twice that week as there was so little to do. Everything was so pleasant and normal. In spite of everything, I felt sorry for him, knowing what was in store for him on Thursday.

When the day finally arrived, I felt slightly sick with nerves as I walked across the field to work; in fact I was so apprehensive that I had contemplated phoning in to say I wasn't well, so much did I dread the thought of what was about to happen, but I decided against it in the end.

There was no sign that anything unusual had taken place during the night, though I could only assume that the boat had made its delivery without any hitch. It was a hazy, autumnal day once again, with pockets of sea-mist blotting out the view of the cliffs. On the way down

I stopped, as I had done so many times before, to take a look at Boscothey before descending the path. I still thought it one of the loveliest houses I had ever seen, more beautiful than ever today, with little veils of mist trailing like gauze and softening its corners.

I found when I arrived there that Delia had already left for London. The morning was quiet, full of totally routine work, the only unusual incident provided by Isobel, who slammed some papers down on my desk and left without a word. She had been out of sorts with me ever since the exchange with Delia in the kitchen; clearly she saw me as Teacher's Pet. Little did she know, I thought now. Maybe she would feel differently by the end of the day.

It was about three in the afternoon when the police came. They were very polite, and Paul, who came out of his office and into mine to greet them, was affability itself at first. With his usual courtesy he ushered them into his inner office, not revealing any sign of panic though he must surely have suspected that all was far from well. When they all came out again, he looked shocked and pale.

'There's been some terrible mistake, Prue,' he said, pausing for a moment beside my desk. 'But don't worry. It'll all be cleared up in no time. Keep things ticking over, there's a good girl.'

Max came into the office about ten minutes later. I turned to him, expecting him to look relieved, but to my surprise he seemed furiously angry – with himself, I soon found out.

'I think we've blown it,' he said bitterly. 'The chef's done a runner. He must have seen us and taken fright.'

'But he can't have!' I said. 'I saw him only a minute ago.' I went swiftly over to the window from where I had a good view of the courtyard and the kitchen beyond it.

'Look – you can see right into the kitchen from here. And there's Gaston. See for yourself.'

There could be no mistake. There was Gaston quite close to the window, wearing his high chef's hat and gesticulating wildly to someone out of vision.

'Not that one,' Max said a little testily, having come to stand behind me. 'It's the other one we want. The pretty boy. Beaumont. He's the real villain.'

'*Sean?*' I swivelled round and stared at him in astonishment. 'Are you sure?'

'Oh, yes,' Max said. 'I'm sure all right.'

Why was I so surprised, I asked myself? Because he looked the way he did? I knew him to be a liar, after all, and something of a conman, at least where Mandy was concerned. But a drug dealer – maybe a murderer?

'Could he be the one who killed Jodie?' I asked.

Max's expression was grim, his eyes flinty.

'I'd bet my pension on it,' he said.

Ten

I still found it difficult to take in.
'But you told me it was the French chef you wanted.'

'Sean Beaumont's French. At least, his father is. His mother's Irish. He lived in Dublin over a pub for the first twelve years of his life, but then the whole family moved to Paris.'

'He told me it was his father who was Irish – the son of a lord with a castle in Tipperary!'

'And you believed him?' He looked cynically amused.

'Well, at first I did,' I admitted, feeling a complete idiot. 'I told myself that someone had to be a lord, and he sounded so plausible. It was only later when I knew first-hand he was a liar that I began to doubt.'

'It sounds as if he's a chip off the old block,' Max said. 'Far from being a member of the aristocracy, Beaumont's father is a real low-life – a convicted conman among many other things.'

'I thought it was Gaston you wanted. Sean told me he had some kind of police record.'

'That's true, but it was a relatively minor offence. A touch of embezzlement – money he swore he intended to repay when circumstances allowed, which of course might or might not be the truth. Even so, he's been clean for a long time now and at worst he had nothing to touch the Beaumonts' form, *père et fils*. Sean might be young

149

but he's experienced, believe me. Experienced and evil. Well, he can't have got far.'

He left me then; left me to think of a hundred questions I should have asked – like was Paul actually being arrested, and if so, was he likely to be allowed out on bail? Should I ring Head Office and inform them what had happened, so that they could send another manager? What should I say to the rest of the hotel staff? And what exactly was happening to Delia? Presumably she, too, would be taken into custody once she had arrived in London and made her delivery.

Then there was the matter of this enormous wedding that we were organising. It was only fair to the parties involved to let them know if the whole thing was likely to be cancelled at short notice.

I put these and other matters to Carol and Marcia Willis, who both converged in my office, round-eyed and full of questions, once Paul had left with the police.

They were questions I hesitated to answer, not knowing how much to tell or where to start. That was something else I should have asked Max. Was I absolved of all vows of secrecy now?

'Paul's suspected of something,' I said at last. 'Smuggling, I think. He told me to keep things ticking over, but I don't quite know what to do.'

'Nothing, yet,' Marcia said decisively. 'None of the guests are around to see anything's amiss. We'll do as he says: keep going until things become clearer. I'm sure he'll be back soon. If you ask me, the whole thing's a mistake. Can you really imagine Paul being *positive* enough to be involved in anything illegal?'

Carol and I said nothing, but were probably both thinking the same thing. Under Delia's thumb, he was likely to do anything she demanded. However, I was glad to have the responsibility taken out of my hands by an older and much more experienced member of staff, and readily agreed to do nothing for the moment. I wished, most sincerely, that I could share her pious hope that Paul would be found to be the victim of some police misunderstanding, but I didn't see how this could be possible.

'What about Sean?' she asked. She had been about to leave the room but turned at the door as the thought struck her. 'Is he anything to do with this? He hasn't been around since this morning. Mandy's distraught, and Gaston wants his guts for garters.'

'The police seem to think he is.'

'Oh, my God! We're in for trouble,' she said as she left the room. 'Gaston will go berserk.'

The scene this remark conjured in the imagination was, indeed, frightful, but it seemed to be the least important aspect of the situation. Gaston, like the rest of us, would have to put up with an entirely changed hotel; that is, if it survived at all.

I felt angry, most of all with Sean. He had everything going for him: ability, looks, personality. He even had the burning ambition that could have taken him to the top if he'd worked hard and followed the course that most successful restaurateurs had taken before him. Instead, he had to lie and cheat – and even, maybe, kill – to further his objectives, for I had no doubt that his aim was to make money at all costs to further his career. I wondered where he had gone, and hoped very much that the police had caught up with him. Nothing, in my view, was bad enough for him if he turned out to be Jodie's killer.

I collected Jamie from the farm after work, as always, and found that he hadn't been too well that day. Grace assured me that in her opinion it was nothing serious – otherwise, she said, she would have phoned me. It was just a bit of a cold, she thought, and a slightly raised temperature. Children were like that – their temperatures went up and down at the drop of a hat. She advised bed and Calpol. Still I worried, as I felt his forehead and looked into his feverish eyes and he clung to me and snivelled into my neck when I picked him up.

'If he's no better tomorrow, maybe he should see a doctor,' Grace said.

I wouldn't hesitate, I assured her, and took him home. It was a grey, miserable afternoon, mist creeping in from the sea, and I was glad to get him indoors – and glad, too, that Ian wasn't coming over, as I felt sure I was in for a disturbed evening. His senior partner was on the verge of retiring and there was going to be a dinner in Truro to mark the occasion. Ian was to give a speech and make a presentation, so his presence was essential, but he had said that he would ring me before it all started so that he could hear how the day's events at the hotel had gone.

Jamie refused his supper but drank some milk and took his dose of medicine. He went to sleep almost at once, but as I stood looking down at him in his cot I could see that it wasn't his usual peaceful sleep. He was flushed and breathing heavily, moving his head restlessly from time to time. I stopped being glad that Ian wasn't with me. This, I thought with alarm, is the sort of occasion when you need someone else to turn to – someone who would give a second opinion and help make decisions. Should I phone the doctor there and then? I couldn't make up my mind. It seemed the kind of fever that could quite well be gone by morning; on the other hand, it might be the beginning of something serious. How on earth was I to know?

Ian, when he rang, said if there was any doubt in my

mind at all, then I should phone the doctor. 'I wish I could be there with you,' he said.

'So do I!'

'I could scrub this party. Jim could give the speech as well as me; better, probably.'

'Don't be daft! Of course it must be you. I'm sure we'll be all right, Ian. Honestly. I don't suppose it's anything serious. Kids do this all the time. You'll learn!'

'Well, if he gets any worse, phone the doctor at once,' he said. 'And Prue – take care of yourself, too. I'll see you tomorrow.'

'I hope the speech goes well.'

'I just wish I didn't have to do it. Not tonight. I'd rather be with you. I happen to love you.'

I believed him. He'd shown it in so many ways, and for a moment I felt comforted, as if in such a wonderful world, so full of promise, there couldn't possibly be anything serious the matter with Jamie. When I went up to look at him once more after I'd had my supper, he seemed to be breathing a little easier, much to my relief.

Later, after it was dark, I looked again and was bending over the cot, tucking in the blanket a little more firmly, when I heard a sound from downstairs. It was the creak of the back door; I recognised it instantly and in that moment realised that for once in my life I hadn't shot the bolts, as I always did if I knew I wasn't going out again. Normally it was routine, an automatic action, but that night I had been so concerned about Jamie that I'd forgotten it when I first came home and it had slipped my mind ever since.

The area surrounding the cottage was so quiet that inside the slightest noise was audible. For a second I stood there listening, not daring to breathe. Again I heard a noise – just the faint scrape of a footstep on the stone flags of the kitchen. Someone was downstairs; there was no doubt of it.

For a moment I couldn't move, shocked into panic. If I stayed quiet, I thought, maybe whoever it was downstairs would go. But then I changed my mind. It wasn't in my nature to let any intruder violate my living space.

Silently I crossed over to my own bedroom and extracted an old hockey stick from the back of an eaves cupboard, the repository for all kinds of junk. Creeping to the staircase, I heard again the scrape of a shoe, and gripping the hockey stock in the middle I crept noiselessly down the stairs.

Burglary wasn't common in these parts, and in any case I had nothing anyone would want to steal – except my precious pictures by Bagley, of course. Someone might know about that.

Kit knew. The thought made me catch my breath and pause halfway down the stairs. If he were truly broke, as Ian had implied, he might have come back to get them. He would know just how much they were likely to make on the open market.

A visit from him was a dreaded possibility that had lurked at the back of my mind ever since he left, and in that moment, my heart plummeting, I was convinced that it had actually happened.

I straightened up and took a deep breath, determined to confront him. I thought it would put me at an advantage if I took him by surprise, so I went downstairs cautiously. There was no sign of anyone in the sitting room, but the light in the kitchen was off even though I knew quite well I had left it switched on.

Sheer anger made me feel all-powerful. How dared he come in like this, as if I still owed him something and he had every right to be here? If he thought he could intimidate me now just as he had done in the past, then he was wrong. I was a different person now.

For a second I stood at the foot of the stairs, listening. I could hear nothing, but even so I knew he was still there. The sense of an alien presence was unmistakable.

Suddenly spoiling for action, I crossed to the kitchen doorway and snapped on the light, to see that there was indeed a masculine figure beside the window. He had pulled the curtain aside and had clearly been peering outside into the mist that now surrounded the cottage, until the shock of the light that flooded the kitchen made him drop the curtain and whip around to face me.

Not Kit, but Sean. Of course, it would be. It seemed so obvious now. He smiled at me; that old, charming, familiar smile.

'Hi, Prue. How are you this lovely evening? And what do you propose to do with that lethal weapon you're brandishing in my direction? Scare the living daylights out of me?'

I slackened my grip and the hockey stick drooped.

'I thought you were long gone,' I said coldly, not returning the greeting. 'What are you doing here?'

'Well now, sweetheart, what do you think?'

'Hiding from the police, I imagine. You know they're looking for you?'

'Of course I do.' He took a step towards me, still smiling, and lifted his hands helplessly. 'It's all a mistake, Prue, I promise you. I've known about the Ransleighs' smuggling sideline for ages and it came as no surprise to me when the police took Paul away this morning – it was something I'd been expecting for a long time – but believe me, I had nothing to do with it.'

'Why did you run, then?'

'Sheer panic!'

'No reason to panic if you're innocent.'

'Really?' He laughed. 'You really believe that? What a sweet little innocent you are.' His smile was rueful now, like a little boy caught with his hand in the cookie jar. 'Where drugs are concerned – well, let's say I've got form. Oh, I've done nothing a million other kids haven't done before me. I was caught at Customs once with just enough cannabis on me for my own use, that's all – it wasn't that I was a pusher, or they found any hard drugs. Nothing like that. Nowadays nobody would have bothered, but this happened way back and there it is – I've got a police record. I knew if they caught me they'd fit me up, but I'm totally innocent. I mean, for God's sake –' he spread his arms wide and laughed – 'do I *look* like a criminal?'

Intellectually, I didn't believe a word of it but I had to remind myself that he was a proved and practised liar, so plausible did he sound.

'I'm not sure I know what criminals look like,' I said. 'But whether you're guilty or not, you can't stay on the run. They'll find you in the end. It would probably go much better for you if you turned yourself in.'

'Oh, yes? You think so? Well, bless your innocent, darlin' little heart! I'm afraid I don't agree with you.' He pulled out a chair, sat down at the kitchen table and winked at me. 'Now how about giving the poor misguided fugitive a cup of coffee?'

I looked at him stonily. Maybe he'd forgotten that I had ceased to be beguiled by him a long time ago.

'I want you to go, Sean,' I said.

'With not so much as a kind word and a hot drink? Ah now, you wouldn't grudge me that, surely?'

For a second I hesitated. I wanted nothing more than for him to leave so that I could lock the door behind him, but neither did I want to antagonise him. After all, Max had seemed sure that this was the man who killed Jodie.

After Jodie

It was hard to analyse the latent menace I could feel, for his smile was as beguiling as ever, but I felt sure it wasn't a product of my imagination. I went and filled the kettle in the hope that once he'd had his coffee he would go.

'I hope you don't mind instant,' I said.

He laughed at that. 'Well, it's hardly up to my usual standard, sweetheart, but under the circumstances I'll put up with it.'

Neither of us spoke as we waited for the kettle to boil. When the coffee was ready I put the mug on the table beside him.

'Drink up and go,' I said unsmilingly.

He looked up at me, the smile fading as if he had at last realised that his charm was lost on me. His eyes and lips had narrowed and hardened and the sheer dislike in his eyes was chilling.

'My dear Prue,' he said. 'You have been a pain in the arse ever since you blessed us all with your presence. Sure I'll go – but when I'm good and ready.' He took a sip of the coffee and pulled a face. 'Haven't you got a drop of anything stronger to help this muck go down?'

'I'm afraid not.'

'Too virtuous to be true, aren't you? Just like your dear little friend Jodie, God rest her soul.'

I didn't rise to this but sat down at the table opposite him, leaning towards him a little.

'Sean,' I said, trying to speak softly and persuasively. 'You're an intelligent kind of guy. You must know in your heart that giving yourself up is the only option that makes sense. You can't hide for ever and you'll be found in the end.'

'And am I to rely on your wonderful judicial system for a fair trial?' He gave a short, derisive laugh. 'It can't have escaped your notice that I'm Irish. If you think I'd get fair treatment from an English court, then you're a fool.'

'You're wrong. Anyway, you can't stay here.'

'I said I would go, didn't I? I just need a little bit of help from you, that's all.'

'I can't help you. And you can only help yourself by going to the police.'

He thumped the table with his fist and leaned towards me, his mouth contorted with anger.

'Will you ever shut up about that? I'm not going, and that's an end of it. Now, what I want you to do is to go to the hotel and get me the keys of the *Firefly*. You know exactly where they are.'

I stared at him.

'You're crazy! The place is locked up at this time of night. Anyway, the police might be there for all I know.'

'Benny will come if you ring the bell. He won't have gone to bed yet. And if anyone asks questions you can say you've come to get something you left behind – your mobile phone, maybe.'

'There's no fuel in the boat. I know that for a fact.'

He appeared to think this over.

'OK,' he said. 'Plan B. You can also get me the keys of the Peugeot so I can pick up some cans from the store. Don't know why I didn't think of it before. I shall need plenty of fuel where I'm going.'

'And where might that be?'

'Where else but Ireland? In the first instance, anyway. Then who knows where? Somewhere far beyond the reach of the local Plods.'

'Of course. The land of your fathers – in the hope that your grandfather will get you out of trouble? Lord Whatsisname of Wherever? Or is he dead? I can't quite remember.'

I knew I shouldn't have said it the moment the ill-considered words were out of my mouth, though it wasn't so much the words themselves as the way I spoke that gave away my total disbelief in his fantasies. He shot out a hand and grabbed my forearm.

'You don't believe me?' he said, in a way that frightened me.

I looked at him without speaking, knowing it would be sensible to assure him that of course I believed every word that fell from his lips. Somehow I couldn't do it.

'I—' I began, and stopped.

'I hope you're not calling me a liar, Prue,' he said softly.

I looked at him in bewilderment. Had he fooled even himself with his lies? I'd heard this was possible; and if it were so in Sean's case, it seemed to me that he could be dangerously unbalanced.

'I wouldn't do that,' I said.

'My grandfather is a peer of the realm.'

'Of course.'

My insincerity must have been obvious, my answer too quick, too glib.

'You little bitch,' he said. 'I'll not be called a liar, by you or anyone.'

'It hardly matters what I believe, does it? It doesn't affect your present situation.'

It was at this moment that I heard Jamie begin to cry. I pulled my arm away and instantly got to my feet so that I could go to him, but Sean, too, was out of his chair in a flash and holding me back with a grip like iron.

'Let me go, Sean,' I said. 'My little boy's crying. He's ill.'

'Leave him.'

'I can't do that. He's ill, I tell you.'

'I'll go.'

'No! He'll be frightened. It's me he wants.'

'I'll go,' he repeated. He was smiling again now, but it wasn't the charming smile everyone was accustomed to. 'I mean it,' he said softly. To my horror I realised that he had reached into his pocket and produced a small, snub-nosed gun which he was pointing in my direction. I stared at it in disbelief.

'Put that thing away! What do you think you're doing? Have you gone crazy?'

'Not at all.' Still smiling, he was very controlled and as cold as ice. 'Just making sure you do things my way.'

'I must go to Jamie.'

His eyes darted this way and that as he appeared to be thinking over a plan of action.

'OK. Go to him. Just know that I'll be right behind you.'

I turned and ran upstairs to where a tearful Jamie was sitting up in his cot, the picture of misery, his nose running, his hands knuckling his eyes. He looked at me reproachfully.

'You didn't come,' he said.

'I'm sorry, darling.' I wiped his nose and felt his forehead. For all his distress, I thought he seemed a little better.

Sean had stayed in the shadows outside the door, but now he showed himself.

'Pick him up,' he said. I did so.

'Who's that man?' Jamie asked, the residue of his tears still causing a few hiccups. He craned his head round my shoulder to take a look at Sean.

'Just a friend,' I said. I prayed he hadn't noticed the gun, but at this Sean raised it a little, pointing it at Jamie.

'Give him to me,' he said.

'No!' I turned my back on him, shielding Jamie from him but looking anxiously over my shoulder.

'Hand him over!'

He took a step towards us and roughly manhandled Jamie out of my arms. Jamie was crying again and so was I by this time, though I was doing my best to stay calm for his sake.

'Don't you dare hurt him.'

'Entirely up to you, sweetheart.' Sean was smiling again. He put the gun to Jamie's head. '*Now* will you go and get the keys?'

I tried to get my voice and my breathing under control. It was difficult, for Jamie was crying pathetically and holding out his arms to me.

'Sean, let's be reasonable about this,' I said, taking a step or two towards him. 'I don't think it's going to work. Suppose the police are at the hotel? OK, I can spin my tale about leaving something behind, but what happens if they come into the office with me? They're not going to let me take any keys away.'

'I didn't realise you were so negative,' he said. 'Oh, for God's *sake*,' he said, suddenly losing patience. 'Can't you shut this kid up?'

'He's frightened. He wants me.'

'Well, take him. Put some clothes on him. We'll have to take him with us.'

I took Jamie into my arms, murmuring soothing words to him.

'It's all right, darling. Don't cry. I'm here.'

'We're taking you for a walk,' Sean said. Jamie put his thumb in his mouth and turned round, his sleepy eyes full of bewilderment. Sean jerked his gun. 'Go on,' he said to me. 'Get him dressed.'

'He's not well,' I said again. 'It's cold and damp out there. I don't want to take him outside.'

'He'll live,' Sean said. 'At least he will if you do what you're told.'

I looked at him helplessly and didn't argue any more. I dressed Jamie warmly, speaking to him reassuringly, and rather to my surprise he seemed to perk up a little, diverted by the thought of going out in the dark. He didn't appear to have registered the fact that Sean was standing over us both with a gun in his hand; perhaps he thought it was a toy. I hoped that he did.

Once he was dressed, Sean indicated with another jerk of the gun that we were go to downstairs. I put Jamie into his anorak and wellies, put on my own jacket, and we began our walk.

Mist was swirling in from the sea, making everything unfamiliar. Sheep loomed up at us from time to time, skittering away in our presence. Even though I knew the path like the back of my hand it was hard to keep to it, for there were a number of tracks going off in different directions and it was easy to get disorientated.

We didn't go fast enough for Sean's liking. Jamie stumbled from time to time, and after a while wouldn't walk any more, clinging to me and asking to be carried.

'He's still sleepy,' I said to Sean. 'He's had some medicine.'

'Pick him up then.'

I did so, but with him in my arms I couldn't keep up the pace Sean demanded and eventually he took Jamie from me and, indicating that I was to go ahead of him, told me to get a move on. There was nothing else I could do. He had my son and he had a gun.

As I walked, I was fighting my overwhelming panic, trying desperately to think clearly. I couldn't believe that Sean's plan would work and I was terrified that the whole thing would end in tragedy. But before then, there would come a point when we had to split up – when Sean, presumably, would conceal himself and Jamie while I attempted to get the keys. Surely then there would be a chance for me to sound the alarm? I could make a phone call – even, I supposed, explain the situation to Benny, though I didn't give much for my chances of being able to make him understand that some swift action was necessary.

But all the time I was in there, Sean would have Jamie as a hostage. I didn't dare to do anything that would put him in any greater danger.

'They might have staked out *Firefly*,' I said over my shoulder.

'I've thought of—' he began, then stopped, reaching out to pull me to a halt. We could hear voices somewhere to our right, disembodied, almost ghostly.

'. . . the beach,' I heard someone say. 'High tide . . .'

We had just gone through a gap in a small clump of stunted bushes and Sean pushed me into their shelter. Jamie whimpered and for a moment, as the mist shifted a little, I could see two indistinct figures walking away from us towards the coastal path. They had obviously heard nothing, or, if they had heard a sound, had attributed it to the sheep.

'There's two pigs who won't be at the hotel,' Sean said in my ear. 'You did well not to call out. Don't ever forget I've got a gun. Remember, if you try anything, to use a somewhat corny phrase, the kid gets it. Believe me, I wouldn't hesitate.'

I stayed quite still for a moment, not obeying his order to get moving.

'It was you who killed Jodie, wasn't it.' I said. It was a statement, not a question, for I had no doubt now that Max was right. Sean was evil and ruthless and I felt nothing but revulsion for him. And this was the man I had to leave holding my son while I carried out his plan for escape.

'No one else had the guts,' he said. 'I'd do it again.

Sure, I might have to do it tonight if you don't do what you're told. Get a move on now.' He prodded me in the back with the gun and I stumbled off, taking the path that led down to the hotel, though momentarily the mist thickened again and I felt as if I were going down into a void.

Suddenly I could hear the hollow, booming note of the St Venn lighthouse. It must have been sounding all the time, but only now had the wind shifted so that it reached us.

'It's not the night for a boat trip,' I said. 'You'll end up on the rocks.'

'Shut up and keep walking. Nothing's going to stop me. You'd better believe it. *Keep walking!*'

This last directive was to counter my sudden halt, for the wind that had brought us the sound of the foghorn had shifted the mist too, and now the hotel could be seen. The mist obscured the ground floor, but with the lights blazing upstairs it looked like a ship riding the ocean.

Once down in the grounds, Sean directed me away from the guests' car park round to the back yard. The hotel vehicles were kept under a kind of carport – the little minibus with the name of the hotel on the side, the Saab and the Peugeot. Now, of course, only the bus and the Peugeot were there as Delia had taken the newer, faster Saab to London. Jamie, I was thankful to see, had dropped off to sleep, his head lolling awkwardly over Sean's shoulder.

'We'll wait in the shed, me and the kid,' Sean murmured in my ear. 'Try the kitchen door. It might be open.'

'It won't be.'

'*Try it.*'

It was, as I thought, securely locked.

'Go round to the front, then, and ring the bell.'

'Suppose Benny doesn't hear—'

'Do it. Now. I'll give you five minutes to get in and out – and don't even *think* of telling anyone where I am.'

'Five minutes? It might take that long for Benny to open the door – and suppose there is a policeman inside? He'd want to speak to me, ask why I'm there—'

'And just suppose,' Sean whispered, sounding almost pleasant, 'that you come back and find your baby dead? He's asleep. He wouldn't know a thing. Just get on with the job and shut up. Five minutes, I said.'

I raced off, round to the front steps. I pressed the bell that was set in the stonework, but could hear nothing. I hoped it was ringing loud and clear in the little cubby-hole at the back where Benny spent his nights, but he seemed in no hurry to answer it and I pressed it again.

After what seemed the longest few minutes I had ever experienced he unlocked the door. He was dishevelled, his shirt collar undone, his jacket hanging open, and was not best pleased to see me.

'Do 'ee know the time, maid?' he said gruffly, peering out at me. 'What you'm doin' 'ere?'

I pushed past him and raced to the office, throwing disjointed explanations over my shoulder as I did so.

'Sorry, Benny – must get – it's my phone, you see – emergency—'

I glanced at my watch as I ran. Three minutes already! Surely Sean would give me a moment's grace? I couldn't possibly have been any faster. Taking the key of the cabinet from my desk, I unlocked it with shaking fingers, my breath rasping in my throat, and grabbed the two sets of keys from their hooks, succeeding in my haste in dropping both of them to the floor. Desperately I scrabbled on the carpet to get them and raced out to the hall again, where Benny was standing looking in my direction with his mouth open and a look of total astonishment on his face.

''Tis all panic and upset around 'ere,' he complained as I fled past him. 'I don't know what the world's coming to.'

'I'll explain tomorrow,' I said as I ran down the steps, leaving him framed in the doorway, scratching his head.

How long had I been? I'd never run so fast, down the steps, round the side of the hotel, back to the yard.

'You took your time,' Sean said, detaching himself from the shadow of the shed as I pounded up to him. My relief was so great at seeing that Jamie was still asleep on his shoulder, I almost collapsed. 'I've located the cans of fuel, just inside the door. Put them in the car.'

Without argument but panting helplessly, I went to the back of the Peugeot, but I couldn't find the keyhole that would enable me to unlock the tailgate. For a moment I fumbled, while Sean stood over me and swore.

'Get the fucking thing opened,' he hissed. Dark though it was, I could see the gleam of the pistol as he jerked it towards me.

'I'm *trying*!' I was almost sobbing by this time. 'Don't you think I want to get this over?'

'God – *women!*' He shifted the gun to his left hand. 'I suppose I'll have to—'

'Drop the gun,' a voice shouted behind him, and all at once there were lights blazing and figures racing towards us. I could see Sean's white, wild face suddenly illuminated as he twisted around, Jamie slipping sideways in his loosened grasp. Seizing my chance, I made a grab for him, just as two policemen laid hold of Sean and took the gun out of his hand.

Two seconds. Maybe three. That's all it had taken, and now it was over. Unable to speak or to think – unable to do anything but hold Jamie close – I leaned trembling against the car. A figure emerged from the shadows surrounding the outbuildings as Sean was hustled away. It was Max. And then, pounding across the gravel, another figure raced to my side and pulled both Jamie and me into his arms.

It was Ian, and he was as unable to speak coherently as I. It didn't matter. The closeness and the awareness that we were safe would suffice for the moment.

'Sorry you went through so much,' Max said when at last we drew apart. Jamie had woken up and was rubbing his eyes, whimpering rather peevishly at all the disturbance. 'We had you both in our sights from the moment you arrived here, but that was the first chance we had to get him without putting your little boy in danger. It was the first time he dropped his guard for a second.'

'It couldn't have been easy,' I said. 'Just waiting.'

Max laughed. 'Taking Beaumont was easy,' he said. 'Keeping your Sir Galahad here from charging across was the difficult part.'

I turned to Ian.

'What are you doing here anyway?' I asked him. 'You're supposed to be in Truro.'

'I said my piece and left early,' he said. 'I was worried. I nearly went crazy when I found you gone and the cottage wide open. I thought Jamie must be really ill and you'd taken him to the hospital – and then the phone rang and it was Max—'

'Just checking,' Max interrupted. 'I had this hunch that Beaumont would contact you and I couldn't get it out of my head. So when Ian told me you weren't anywhere to be found, I collected him and we tore down here.'

'How did you know he'd bring me here?'

'We didn't, not for sure. But we'd thought about the boat. It seemed more than likely that he'd try to get hold of it and would need the keys, if he didn't already have them. We weren't sure about that, so we've got St Venn harbour staked out, too. He'd never have got away.'

'He admitted he killed Jodie.'

Ian put his arms round me again.

'You've had a hell of a time,' he said. 'I don't think I'll ever be able to let you out of my sight again.'

'*Eem!*' It was as if Jamie had only now woken enough to realise that Ian was present, and there was a comical note of surprise and delight in his voice. He sounded brighter, as if a walk in the mist was the perfect remedy for a feverish cold. It was enough to break the tension and make us all laugh a little.

'Come on,' Ian said, taking him from me. 'It's time we got this young man home to bed. He's had enough excitement for one night.'

'He's not the only one,' I said.

For a moment he held me within the circle of his arm, my small son against his other shoulder, and I leaned my head against him, overwhelmed suddenly by the reassurance I felt in his presence – my lover, my friend, my rock.

I felt safe, and exactly where I was meant to be. Yet I knew that I was on the brink of something not only safe but exciting – even challenging. Life was like that; marriage certainly was, and I had the scars to prove it.

But this was no moment for details. The whole future lay ahead, for me and for Jamie. And it felt so good.